THE CHEERL]

"One of the truest portraits of an American girl ever written"

—*Detroit Free Press*

"It's heartbreaking at times, hilarious at others."

—*Philadelphia Inquirer*

"Utterly honest, accurate, and sympathetic."

—*Kansas City Star*

"A classic."

—*Publishers Weekly*

SNOWY

"MacDougall's sexy, painfully true story illuminates what an endless process growing up is."

—*Booklist*

"Readers should prepare to laugh out loud and cry in earnest as former high school cheerleader Henrietta Snow grows up in this delightful sequel to *The Cheerleader* . . . Highly recommended."

—*Library Journal*

HENRIETTA SNOW

"MacDougall's perspective is generous, accepting and forgiving . . . Funny, sad, unsentimental and wise, *Henrietta Snow* is a delight.

—Rebecca P. Sinkler,
former editor of the *New York Times Book Review*

THE HUSBAND BENCH, *or* BEV'S BOOK

A BORN MANIAC, *or* PUDDLES'S PROGRESS

A GUNTHWAITE GIRL (A NOVELETTE)

SITE FIDELITY

LAZY BEDS

## ALSO BY RUTH DOAN MACDOUGALL

THE LILTING HOUSE
THE COST OF LIVING
ONE MINUS ONE
WIFE AND MOTHER
AUNT PLEASANTINE
THE FLOWERS OF THE FOREST
A LOVELY TIME WAS HAD BY ALL
A WOMAN WHO LOVED LINDBERGH
MUTUAL AID

### The Snowy Series

THE CHEERLEADER
SNOWY
HENRIETTA SNOW
THE HUSBAND BENCH, or BEV'S BOOK
A BORN MANIAC, or PUDDLES'S PROGRESS
A GUNTHWAITE GIRL (a novelette)
SITE FIDELITY

### With Daniel Doan

50 HIKES IN THE WHITE MOUNTAINS
50 MORE HIKES IN NEW HAMPSHIRE

### Editor

INDIAN STREAM REPUBLIC:
SETTLING A NEW ENGLAND FRONTIER,
1785–1842, by Daniel Doan

To Nancy —
with gratitude,
Ruth

# *Lazy Beds*

by

Ruth Doan MacDougall

A sequel to:

THE CHEERLEADER

SNOWY

HENRIETTA SNOW

THE HUSBAND BENCH, or BEV'S BOOK

A BORN MANIAC, or PUDDLES'S PROGRESS

A GUNTHWAITE GIRL (a novelette)

SITE FIDELITY

FRIGATE BOOKS

At the author's website, ruthdoanmacdougall.com, items of general interest such as discussion guides, background information, and photographs are available.



Cover photograph:
Robert J. Kozlow, "Sunrise on Lake Winnipesaukee"

Cover design:
Richard Hannus

Publisher's Cataloging-in-Publication Data
MacDougall, Ruth Doan
Lazy beds / Ruth Doan MacDougall
p.cm
ISBN 13: 978-1-7359716-0-5 (paperback)
ISBN 13: 978-0-9663352-8-6 (e-book)

Women—New Hampshire—Fiction
I. Title Series: Snowy
PS3563.A292L39 2020
813'.54

To Ann Norton Holbrook

# Acknowledgments

For their advice and help, my gratitude to:

Sally Barrett
Terry Brodrick
Amy Brown
Jere Burrows
Lynn Burns Butler
Jennifer Davis-Kay
Penelope Doan
Sandra Gottwald
Hal Graham
Richard Hannus
Thane Joyal
Robert J. Kozlow
Jane Rice
Jan Schor
Steve Smith
Daniel Weene
Marney Wilde

# FOREWORD

"Kerfuffle" is the first word in *Lazy Beds*. As Snowy drives past beautiful Lake Winnipesaukee on a glorious autumn day, in the New Hampshire Lakes Region she's lived in most of her life, she muses about this odd noun's sudden appearance in her head. The old Scots verb "fuffle," to throw into disorder, and "ker," from the Gaelic word "car," to twist or turn around, combine in this delicious, onomatopoeia-like word to mean, basically, "confused ruckus." We then get a snapshot of this moment: "Henrietta Snow Sutherland Forbes was a poet, the owner of three general stores, a new bride as of June, and a first-time grandmother as of August. But on this sunny Sunday afternoon, October 26, 2008, she was mostly feeling like a best friend."

Thus begins the latest novel of Ruth Doan MacDougall's Snowy Series that began in 1973 with the classic bildungsroman *The Cheerleader*. The very specific time frame of *Lazy Beds*—just after the 2008 economic collapse and on into 2009—highlights the kerfuffles in its core storylines: Bev's struggles in creating a bed-and-breakfast out of Waterlight, her beloved lakefront home, and Snowy's challenges in overseeing the three small stores run by family and friends. Yeats's "The Second Coming" haunts Snowy as she contemplates the sometimes overwhelming anxiety they all feel facing myriad losses from the recession, hearing the poem's ominous pronouncements that "[t]hings fall apart; the centre cannot hold" as personal prophecies. This foreboding, though, doesn't curtail the sheer glee Snowy and her fellow Democrats experience when the first Black president is elected and Dudley's son and Snowy's son-in-law D. J. is reelected to the House of Representatives.

Waterlight's remodeling works as a metaphor for the changes they, New Hampshire, and America have experienced. What were once "camps" for middle-class families are now expensive retreats, and those who were comfortable are less so. Bev and Roger, serving affluent vacationers, get an unwitting education in the privilege they've taken for granted and to which they still feel entitled. Bev ruefully comments on Snowy's poetic use of the gardening term "lazy beds," a simple method that entails planting seed potatoes in the soil and then covering them with mulch: "I think of that when I'm making these damn beds that aren't 'lazy' to me, though they are to the guests lolling in them on vacation." "Lazy beds," then, have both literal and ironic meanings here: the hard work catering to tourists that natives Bev, Roger, Snowy, and Ruhamah do in their picturesque Lakes Region towns, and their own search for ways to make their lives and work easier when they can't help feeling that they deserve some retirement relaxation and security, "rocking on [the] porch instead of serving B-and-B guests iced tea there."

As the Gang approaches their golden years, *On Golden Pond*—about an elderly couple's love for their Maine home amidst health emergencies and painful family relations—aptly replaces *Our Town* as a running motif. Fifty-three years earlier, Snowy found *Our Town*'s final graveyard scene "the saddest thing" she had ever heard. Now, watching Bev play a grandmother rather than an ingénue, she can weep "torrents of tears" as Ethel and Norman embrace, saying "good-bye to the lake and the loons," but accept that loss and death are painful because they come with enduring connections to cherished people and places. Snowy adores her grandson, Al, with a "fierce protective love" similar to mother love but "intensified by age, by knowing how much could befall a baby, a child, a human being." Robert Frost, that consummate New Englander, describes in "To Earthward" how in later life he craves "[no] joy but lacks salt / That is not dashed with pain / And weariness and fault . . . "

Snowy's fascination with words and love for language runs throughout, and we see her now confident in her soul's vocation as a poet. Two female New Hampshire and Maine poets continue to inspire Snowy, Celia Thaxter and Edna St. Vincent Millay, and Snowy's own legacy emerges from an unexpected corner: Etta, Bev's younger daughter, has written a mystery novel and shown it to Snowy—in a sense, her literary foremother, as Virginia Woolf would say—rather than to Bev. Here Snowy utters a truth that MacDougall realized early: "If you worried about whether or not your parents and friends would approve of what you wrote (especially sex), you'd never write a word." Snowy—and MacDougall—know that authors have to "toughen [the] heart and conscience, for the sake of art."

In that spirit, MacDougall illustrates unsparingly how age continues, and increases, its assault on these characters we first knew as teenagers who now approach 70. Like any northerner, Snowy takes comfort knowing that beneath winter's snow the plants lie in wait for spring, but remembers that scoliosis "made gardening more pain than pleasure." Bev, looking at *People* magazine, recognizes how little she knows about the contemporary zeitgeist: "nowadays [she] knew hardly anybody except the British royals." When Bev thinks, "How precarious . . . are our lives—and our livelihood; we should be wearing life preservers all the time," she speaks for all of them and all of us. She ponders Snowy's claim "that admitting to limitations was one of the hardest parts of aging," but she also recognizes the hard-won progress women have made and the active lives she and the Gang still enjoy. Contemplating her daughters' choices, she wonders what lies ahead for her granddaughters "now that girls' futures seemed to have boundless possibilities, at least compared with the past . . . " And beautiful Bev may be a grandmother, but her extended family depends on her income from real estate and now the hospitality industry. From these jobs, and from life, she's learned the hard way not to wish for much more than "good coffee," and she has the wisdom to be grateful when the coffee—this one cup now, today—is indeed delectable.

MacDougall exercises again her unerring sense of the comedy in small, ordinary scenes. When Tom and Snowy visit 89-year-old Mildred Cotter in her Maine assisted-living facility, dog-therapy puppies happily run amok, discombobulating the staff but charming the residents. Bev helplessly watches female relatives take over "her" kitchen during a power outage on Christmas Day, and in the chaos a tyrannical three-year-old absurdly but insistently demands dinner, finally appeased by a spoonful of stuffing. This adherence to tradition—so strong that even a toddler expects it—can disappoint or delight, depending on the circumstances. Snowy and Tom, en route to Puddles's Maine home, always stop at the same diner and eat the same food, and this year they relish the experience, but Snowy's pleasure palls as she remembers that last year Tom, suffering from depression and pain following knee replacements, had refused dessert. The currents of old memory and new desire continually intermingle, and MacDougall masterfully shows how this jumbled river runs through all their days.

In the closing chapter, a celebration mixes past, present, and future: the 150th anniversary of the store Snowy and Alan bought twenty-four years earlier, which their daughter continually revives. When Bev marvels that she's known Snowy from "seven to seventy," we can all nod, knowing "how utterly incomprehensible" this feels. Their story is far from over, kerfuffles and all.

Ann Norton Holbrook
Saint Anselm College

# Chapter One

# 1. Snowy

*Kerfuffle*, Snowy thought, turning her Subaru onto Lakeside Road and driving past cottages on Lake Winnipesaukee, the autumn's dark blue water seeming more intense than ever without the competition of bright foliage colors, the leaves of the trees now old gold or rusty brown or fallen. A new septic system at the Inn on East Bay was causing a kerfuffle. Had she ever used that word before, while talking or in a poem? Why had it popped into her head?

Henrietta Snow Sutherland Forbes was a poet, the owner of three general stores, a new bride as of June, and a first-time grandmother as of August. But on this sunny Sunday afternoon, October 26, 2008, she was mostly feeling like a best friend.

Sundays, the Woodcombe General Store closed at noon. Right after she had locked the door behind the last customer and had pulled a fleece vest over her blue Woodcombe General Store sweatshirt, the telephone beside the cash register had rung. Caller ID had told her it was Beverly Lambert's cell phone.

Bev, her best friend, wailed, "Snowy, there's a gigantic gaping hole in the lawn, and creatures are swimming and drowning in it! Frogs, moles, mice, terrible, and Roger just says not to look!"

"Oh, no!" Snowy said. "Why are they drowning?"

"It's too steep for them to climb out, they can't tread water forever! I'm indoors now but I can't stop picturing them! The hole is part of the new septic system, the tank will be delivered tomorrow, supposedly, but meanwhile—Snowy, this is the last straw!"

Snowy realized that over the past few months she'd been too distracted by the pregnancy of Ruhamah, her daughter, and then by the bedazzling charms of her grandson to have paid thorough attention to Bev's plight. She said, "I'll drive down. I haven't seen the renovations, you can show me those. Do you have any guests this weekend?"

"Nobody since the foliage peaked. There's nothing but an awful mess to show you. You mustn't waste your afternoon off—"

Snowy heard Bev gulp back a sob. She reassured, "I'll be there soon," and left the store and hurried up Main Street to the North Country Coffins barn in which she and Tom lived in the apartment over the workshop. After telling him about Bev's meltdown, she drove south out of Woodcombe to Gunthwaite. Her hometown, where she and Bev had met in second grade. Best friends ever since.

Yes, this was her afternoon off. Three years ago Ruhamah had insisted she take Mondays off as well, but this summer Snowy had insisted on working Mondays so that Ruhamah herself could have Mondays free—and whatever other days she felt she needed when the delivery date drew near. Ruhamah had stuck to Mondays but did agree to a maternity leave after the baby's arrival.

Bev's mailbox on Lakeside Road used to be a small one, dented by snowplows, with discreet lettering that said Waterlight. This had been the old name of the big place Bev had bought in 1995, having discovered it during her work as a real-estate agent and getting a good deal on the purchase of what she'd called her dream house. She and Roger, her husband, had been separated for eight years; she was living in a ranch house in Gunthwaite while Roger stayed in their Connecticut home. Into Waterlight she had moved. Five years later Roger had retired from his law practice and moved here without, Snowy gathered, really being formally invited by Bev. Yet they had formally renewed their wedding vows and resumed their life together, for better or worse. During the past year this "worse" happened: the nation's economic crisis; their dwindling savings. Roger had a brainstorm and decided to turn Bev's dream house into a bed-and-breakfast and change its name. After balking, Bev had given in. But there wasn't time to transform the place completely into a business, so this summer they'd only rented two of the three bedrooms with adjoining bathrooms. The third was Bev and Roger's room, which had the best views of the lake from upstairs, and, Bev had told Snowy, she would die before she'd give it up.

The new mailbox's larger lettering said The Inn at East Bay. A strident sign now hung from a tree branch overhead, repeating the new name.

The economy. Last month the stock market had "crashed." Panic seared Snowy as she swung the car down the circular driveway, hearing the lines from Yeats's "Second Coming" that nowadays were pacing heavily through her mind:

> Turning and turning in the widening gyre
> The falcon cannot hear the falconer;
> Things fall apart; the centre cannot hold . . .

Behind the tennis court and brown-shingled garage was an expanse of overturned earth—the leach field?—from which a raw trench disappeared around the right-hand side of the classic summer cottage (winterized long ago) whose brown shingles and green trim blended into the surrounding pines—eek! Snowy braked at the sight of a wooden ramp leading from the driveway to the screened porch, spoiling the look of the entire front of the house.

Bev came rushing off the porch, down the broad stairs, wearing a faded green flannel shirt and old jeans. "I forgot!" she said. "I forgot it's lunchtime, did you have any lunch?"

Snowy clambered out of the car, her back aching. The goddamn scoliosis. Below the lawn on the left side of the house, a lake breeze was jiggling the water around the brown-shingled boathouse and along the small beach. On that lawn Bev and Roger had renewed their vows, Bev in an elegant outfit, a green jacket and green ankle-length skirt to match her eyes, Roger in a navy blazer and gray pants (not intentionally to match his receding gray hair and his gray mustache). She hugged Bev; up close, she could tell that beautiful white-haired Bev had been crying, smudged mascara mingling with exhausted livid puffiness below those green eyes. She replied, "No lunch, but I've been making breakfasts and brunches all morning, nibbling. You and Roger go ahead."

"He's off to the Home Depot, he'll stop at McDonald's. When Parker left Friday after digging the hole for the new tank, he asked us to use as little water as possible over the weekend, so we aren't doing dishes and Roger said I could dash naked through yesterday's rain instead of taking a shower but I certainly did take a shower and today too, though quick. Yesterday's rain! Rain filling up that hole, along with the underground water seeping in, and the poor creatures drowning! I have no appetite."

Snowy remembered Bev had mentioned that Parker Danforth, of Danforth Excavations, was installing the new expanded septic system. The name had lodged in her memory because a sister of her first boyfriend, Ed Cormier, had married a Danforth, and if Ed had lived after being paralyzed in a football game, he would've been Parker's uncle. Hugging Bev again, Snowy said, "I don't want to see the septic hole. Show me what else is new. Is that a handicap ramp?"

"Oh, God, isn't it a ghastly eyesore! Leon built it for us."

Bev and Roger's younger son, Leon, a handyman and the father of Bev's older grandson, Clement, lived with Miranda Flack, Bev's housecleaner, in a mobile-home park across town. Snowy asked, "But a handicap ramp is an essential amenity, isn't it?"

"Roger says we've got to offer everything to everyone, after just making do this summer. TVs and mini-fridges, we've bought them for the bedrooms and stored them in the cellar, waiting for the new bathrooms we're adding, but the contractor and his gang have hardly begun, they've been so busy elsewhere this summer right straight through the foliage season, the carpenters, the flooring man, the tile man, not to mention our plumber—"

Snowy took Bev's arm, as if she herself were the hostess, and led her up the stairs and opened the screen door. The porch circled the house, the front section furnished with four wicker armchairs, their green cushions in need of plumping. Suspended from a ceiling painted sky-blue, a mobile of a black-and-white loon drifted gently, the first loon the B-and-B guests would see of the many loons Bev had collected over the years. The real loons had now migrated from the lake to spend the winter on the ocean.

Bev said, "A welcome mat. Roger says we must get a big welcome mat for the porch. I've seen mats in catalogs that say Go Away. I want one of those."

Snowy tried a lighthearted reminiscence. "Remember the time we saw in some store a mat that said Gone Shopping and we both were tempted to buy it?" She opened the front door and stepped into the large hallway.

Bev had claimed the house was a mess, but the hallway looked normal, and the only change was the presence of Roger's prodigious mahogany desk; on it sat an optimistically thick leather-bound book that identified itself on the cover in gold lettering that Snowy could read without her reading glasses: *Guest Book*. Beside it was a stack of pamphlets. Snowy picked up the top pamphlet, which showed the cruise ship *Mount Washington* plying the waters of Lake Winnipesaukee.

"Roger's idea," Bev said. "He loves telling the guests about all the tourist attractions in the Lakes Region and the White Mountains. I think he tells them more than they want to know."

"Oh, lord," Snowy said, and put the pamphlet down.

Otherwise, the hallway seemed much the same as it had been when Bev had shown Waterlight to her just before buying the place. In the ensuing years Bev had kept the summer souvenirs that had belonged to the original family, the old buoy bolted to one wall, on another wall several taxidermist-preserved fish and also outlines of fish on slabs of wood and pieces of paper, their dates going back to 1920s summers. The family had managed to hold on to the cottage through an earlier stock market crash, in 1929, and the Depression. Decades later, a divorce had finally caused its sale.

Bev said, "I'm sorry, I forgot to ask you how Al is doing. And how are Ruhamah and D. J.? The election is coming fast."

Alan Sutherland Washburn, the most perfect grandson in the whole wide world, was named after Snowy's first husband, Ruhamah's father. Snowy said, "They're all down at Southern New Hampshire University at a rally." Dudley Washburn Jr., Ruhamah's husband and Al's father, was running for reelection to the U.S. House of Representatives. She added, "The tension is always tightening at this phase, and of course this time they have Al on their minds too."

"Mmm," Bev said, obviously not listening. Instead she was looking at the photos on the two other walls as if she'd never seen them before.

Snowy turned, though she herself had certainly seen them often. Over the years Bev had put the accumulating photos of her own family where the original family's photos had hung, and on the dock and the beach, in boats, at the barbecue grill, on the tennis court, there they were: Bev's older son, Dick, and his wife, Jessica, and their little girls, six-year-old Abigail and three-year-old Felicity, who lived in Connecticut; Bev's older daughter, Mimi, and Lloyd, Mimi's graphic-artist husband, who lived near Gunthwaite in Leicester; Bev's younger daughter, Henrietta, nicknamed Etta, and her veterinarian husband, Steve, and their son, two-year-old Jeremy, who lived in Massachusetts. Grandson Clement appeared in photos with Leon and Miranda and, separately, with his mother, Trulianne Hughes, who lived with Clem in an apartment in Bide-a-Wee, the cottage Bev had bought for a real-estate office when she became a realtor.

Bev now seemed to focus on Abigail and Felicity. "Halloween is Friday. Jessica e-mailed me that Abigail is going to be a princess again and Felicity is graduating from being a bumblebee last year to being a butterfly. Jessica will send photos, but I wish I could see the girls in person. Connecticut isn't the far side of the moon, I used to go often, whether or not Roger wanted to accompany me, remember? But Roger says we have to keep our noses to the grindstone."

"You'll see Clem in his costume, won't you?"

"Yes." Bev looked at a photo of Clem and Leon and Miranda. "I forgot to tell you, Miranda says Leon is building a sap house for Clem's school. Last March, Clem got really interested when I took him with me to that farm I always go to for maple syrup. Miranda says he asked his teacher if they could make maple syrup next March, and now they've got the okay, with Leon building a sap house near the woods behind the school. Imagine, next March we'll have been through the winter—*if* we survive."

Snowy asked, "Little kids playing with boiling sap? Is that safe?"

"Not the little kids. The fifth- and sixth-graders. Clem's birthday is a week from tomorrow and he'll be eleven, old enough."

"What Halloween costume has he got this year?"

"A pirate. Remember the year I was a pirate and Mother made my costume? She always made my costumes, and she made that one, eye patch and all."

"I remember," Snowy said, remembering also that Tom did a great imitation of Robert Newton playing Long John Silver in the *Treasure Island* movie. "She even made great big coins out of cardboard and tinfoil, for your treasure."

"Treasure! I wish it were that easy! The septic project is costing thousands! As is everything else!"

## 2. Snowy

"Oh, Bev," Snowy said. Then she asked, "Any changes in the living room?" An elegant staircase soared out of the hallway.

She went past it, past the carved newel posts. To her right and left was the corridor, but she moved straight ahead, under an archway into the vastness of a living room two stories high. The three-sided balcony gave it the feeling of a stage—and how Bev did love a stage! This year Bev had joined the Gunthwaite Summer Theater, whose schedule had ended on the Saturday of Labor Day weekend with a last performance of *On Golden Pond*. Starring Bev as Ethel. Snowy had wept torrents of tears during the last scene as Ethel and Norman embraced and left their cottage, saying good-bye to the lake and the loons.

Following her into the living room, Bev said, "This summer I mostly got away with muffins," so she was thinking of food now, not treasure. "Did I tell you? I made some, but too often I bought them and cinnamon rolls and such at Fay's."

Fay Rollins, a friend of Snowy's who lived in Woodcombe, owned Indulgences, a Gunthwaite bakery. Snowy said, "You're a wonderful cook. Your muffins are scrumptious and so are Fay's, your guests must love them all. And you could introduce your guests to a New England tradition and offer pie for breakfast, the way we do at the store. Pie from Fay's."

"Roger complained that buying from the bakery cuts into profits."

"Oh."

"I don't know how you can make breakfasts and lunches every day at the store."

Sometimes Snowy didn't know either. She surveyed the living room. Over the mantel of the huge fieldstone fireplace was another example of taxidermy art that had come with the place, the antlered head of a moose. The moose had been nicknamed Teddy, for Teddy Roosevelt and the Bull Moose Party. He gazed at the lake out the back wall's French windows, across the four sofas and assorted armchairs and side tables set on assorted rugs, Oriental and braided and hemp. She said, "You haven't changed things here. I didn't think you would have to." Needlepoint loons were swimming across the throw pillows on the sofas. The light that had given the cottage its name struck through the windows with an autumn clarity that made her squint.

"Granola and fruit," Bev said. "Scrambled eggs and omelettes. I've mainly been serving those, trying to keep things comparatively light and simple. One sadistic old man asked for poached eggs. The most difficult eggs to make! Breakfasts themselves are the most difficult meal, aren't they—everything happens at once. *If* we're ready to open for winter guests and *if* anybody comes, they'll want more substantial fare before they go skiing. Oatmeal, pancakes, waffles. I'll have to make my mushroom quiche and—Mimi has offered to help cook and clean, the recession is hurting Weaverbird and she has extra time, but—oh, damn the recession!"

*Things fall apart; the centre cannot hold.* Mimi was a weaver, with a shop named Weaverbird in the Leicester farmhouse she and Lloyd had bought years ago. Hating the thought of another small business in peril, Snowy hurried back to the corridor and peeked in the TV room's doorway at the sofa and armchairs and the large flat-screen TV. "A new TV?"

"Roger said it was a necessity."

Next, at the end of the corridor, came the sitting-room-bedroom-bathroom arrangement that had always been called "the suite." Something else new: a little sign on the door saying Loon Suite in quaint script. Snowy asked, "It has a name now?

"Roger had been studying some B-and-B brochures before writing ours. Most B-and-Bs seem to name their rooms after the views or birds or flowers or mountains or who knows what. He decided on waterfowl, the Loon and the Grebe and the Heron, like the names on the canoes and sailboat that came with Waterlight, and he added more ducks, the Wood Duck and the Merganser, and had Lloyd make the signs."

Snowy said uncertainly, "Hmm." She felt proprietorial about the suite. Back in 1995 Bev had invited her to live here, so she had moved from the Woodcombe General Store's apartment she and Ruhamah shared into the suite, commuting to Woodcombe for eight months before Tom had finally asked her to move in with him. It became a guest suite again, until Roger's arrival; he had turned it into a den with furniture from the Connecticut house. This summer its old furniture had come down from the attic, and it was now the inn's main offering. (The other room Bev and Roger had rented was Leon's old bedroom, off the kitchen, with its own entrance as well as bathroom. Unlike the suite, Leon's bedroom had needed Bev's skills with a paintbrush.) Snowy stepped into the sitting room, where she had worked on her poems while lying on the rattan daybed as well as sitting at her own desk she'd squeezed in, her old mahogany veneer desk she'd had since junior high school.

The bookcase on the suite's secretary type of desk now held New England sightseeing books, not the books she'd brought. She went into the bedroom, where shades had been drawn against the sun on the blue-padded window seat, the blue floral loveseat, the crewel-covered wing chair. The wildflower-sprigged bedspread was new since her occupancy. She had lived in a difficult and bewildering limbo here, Tom's ex-wife visiting Woodcombe too often and not acting ex. Glancing up, she said, "The smoke detector is new."

"Regulations. We have to have them in every bedroom. And we have to have a sprinkler system. Roger's lists go on and on. A locksmith put locks in the bedroom doors. Roger and I have the master key. On and on." Bev straightened a bedside table's cute Baby Ben clock, also new. "Housework! This summer and fall, Miranda and I have only had to remake or change this bed and the one in Leon's old room. And vacuum and dust and tidy and clean the bathrooms. The bathrooms, what people leave behind!" She made the retching noise she'd perfected in high school. "Emptying wastebaskets is disgusting! Would you believe that some people don't wrap a Q-tip in a Kleenex before throwing it away? Well, I did have to teach Roger when we got married. This winter, if we're so-called *lucky*, more bathrooms to clean? More beds! In your 'Lazy Beds' poem you wrote about how it's a gardening term, how it's a Scottish version of raised beds for planting potatoes. I think of that when I'm making these damn beds that aren't 'lazy' to me, though they are to the guests lolling in them on vacation."

Snowy had read that in Gaelic the lazy-beds method of growing potatoes by digging up peat and fertilizing the furrows with seaweed was called *feannagan.* She hadn't used that word in the poem because she didn't know how to pronounce it and neither would her readers. She said sympathetically, "Even making one's own bed every morning is sometimes a challenge."

"And Puddles won't stop joking about how I must be sure to make hospital corners when I change the sheets!"

Jean Pond Cram Hutchinson, nicknamed Puddles, had turned their friendship into a triumvirate when she arrived at Gunthwaite's junior high from Portland, Maine. Now an Advanced Registered Nurse Practitioner, she'd been living in Maine with her second husband these past six years. Snowy said, "She keeps pestering me about when Tom and I will get to Maine."

"Your honeymoon. You were postponing it until after Columbus Day."

Last May, after she had asked Tom to marry her (!) and he had recovered from the shock, they'd talked about honeymooning on Maine's Quarry Island. Snowy said, "Well, there's Al and the election and everything, we keep pushing the date ahead."

"I've been remembering the B-and-Bs we stayed at on ours."

Snowy knew that Bev meant their second honeymoon, when Bev and Roger had gone to Britain for their renewal of vows. "Bed-and-breakfast," Snowy said. "I'd never heard the term until Alan and I went to England."

"In particular I remember one of those honey-colored Cotswold stone houses in Chipping Campden. We stayed there two nights. The owners were in their sixties, and they talked about how they'd converted their home to a B-and-B after the children were grown and gone." Bev left the suite and strode back along the corridor, Snowy scurrying behind. "They'd had a plan," Bev said, "unlike us. The wife ran the B-and-B while the husband kept working at his job, whatever it was, and then when he retired he took over cooking the breakfasts. Full English breakfasts!"

"Fried bread, fried tomatoes?"

"The works." Bev began climbing the staircase.

Snowy followed. "Remember I told you that in the Hebrides Tom and I had the best breakfast at an inn on South Uist, oatmeal-bread toast and kippers and—"

"That Chipping Campden couple were young, in comparison. Roger and I are starting out too old! Seventy-one, sixty-nine! And they knew what they were doing and did it slowly, in an organized fashion. You know why Roger is at the Home Depot? He's decided we should have an outdoor shower so our guests can wash off the sand after swimming on our beach. I pointed out that it's nearly November and people won't be swimming until Memorial Day, if any people should come, but no! Off he went to learn about outdoor showers." She stopped at the top of the stairs. "Regulations—you have to have 'two ways off each floor level,' so the contractor is going to build a fire escape and the work is *supposed* to start by the end of this week. Like the handicap ramp, a fire escape will really embellish the place. At least I convinced Roger to have it built off the back, not the front."

Snowy looked over the balcony railing at the living room below. Teddy the moose was still contemplating the lake.

"Well," Bev said, "here's the start of the mess." Dramatically, she shoved the door of the first room wide open, letting loose a delicate flutter of sawdust. The little sign on the door was: Heron.

This bedroom used to be the only official guest room, aside from the suite. Now the bed had been taken apart, its pieces leaning precariously against a new plastic-wrapped queen-size mattress standing straight up to make room for the stacks of lumber and drywall. Moving down the hall, Bev opened the door to the bedroom that used to be called Etta's (sign: Merganser). A similar scene.

Snowy asked, "Materials for the bathrooms?"

"En suite, as they say in Britain." Bev then marched back along the balcony, past the old non-private upstairs bathroom, to the open door of the room she had made her home office.

Shocked, Snowy saw that its door also had a sign, Wood Duck, and the room was empty of its furnishings. It held the major part of the contractor's materials, supplies, and equipment, including three new gleaming white toilets. Out a window, down in the backyard, a loon whirligig was slowly flapping.

Bev said, "I told you, didn't I, that Roger decreed this room be used for guests? After all, he was giving up his den."

Snowy exclaimed, "No, Bev, you did not tell me! Where's your stuff?" She dashed to Bev and Roger's bedroom (no sign), and there, crammed into Bev's décor of white walls, organdy curtains like clouds, blue rag rugs, a white duvet on the white-painted king-size bed, loons on the pillows, were Bev's antique slant-top desk, her modular computer desk, her filing cabinets, her bookcase. The sofa bed for overflow company. Bev's office had also been her gym: a treadmill, a TV, exercise videos and DVDs, and a rolled-up mat. Bev and Roger's bedroom was the largest in the house, but there was barely room to swing a cat.

Snowy fiercely wanted to see Roger swinging at the end of a hangman's noose.

Bev said, "Roger says I should give up the idea of a home office and just use my office at Bide-a-Wee." She wriggled around the furniture and plopped down in the chair at the slant-top desk. "But what if I have to give up Bide-a-Wee?"

Snowy sank onto the sofa bed. Yankee reticence about finances! She had no idea of what size mortgages Bev owed on Bide-a-Wee and Waterlight. Bev had mentioned getting a good deal on Bide-a-Wee too. But what did that really mean? Bev had bought Bide-a-Wee because the property included a small engine repair shop, with which she had proceeded to lure Clem's mother, a mechanic, along with Clem himself, to Gunthwaite. So besides being Trulianne and Clem's home, it was Trulianne's workplace as well as Bev's. Snowy said, "Give up Bide-a-Wee?"

"The contractor has his own painter," Bev said, switching the subject. "That's the one job I wouldn't've minded doing, painting the new bathrooms. And it would've saved us the cost of the painter. But that's not the deal. At least I was allowed to choose the colors. Colors. Red hair! Remember when I saw on TV that scientists are finding out that redheads feel pain differently?"

Bev had been a redhead. Snowy said, "You reported to me that redheads are a mutant or something."

"I guess I'm feeling pain every which way since Roger took control. Losing my office—the drownings in the septic hole—" Bev jumped up from the desk. "Why am I whining? How heartless! You, Snowy, after Alan—after Alan died, you had to give up your entire house, your Hurricane Farm, the barn and garden and woods, and go live over the store!"

"That was a long time ago."

"I *have* been having fun. I bought hair dryers for all the bathrooms, infuriating Roger who didn't see why that's a nice touch. I've got them stored in our closet along with soaps. Soaps are fun." Then Bev burst into tears.

Bumping into furniture, Snowy rushed for the box of Kleenex on Bev's bedside table. She hugged Bev and thought: kerfuffle? This is far more than a kerfuffle.

## 3. Bev

EARLY FRIDAY MORNING BEV HURRIED FROM THE HOUSE TO THE garage, stowed her laptop and her woven shoulder bag in her green Subaru Outback, and sped off to work, taking shortcuts from Lakeside Road to North Road. Early, yes, but because Roger had insisted on going over some of the scribbled notes on his damn clipboard and legal pad, not so early as she'd planned. Today was

Halloween and she wanted to make sure she got to Bide-a-Wee in time to see Clem in his costume before he boarded the school bus—and to show him the costume she was wearing, even though she was just recycling last year's because she didn't dare spend money on a new one. She'd always created some sort of Halloween costume to wear at the office. Today's consisted of black watch plaid slacks and, under her jacket, a white blouse with a Peter Pan collar, a 1950s outfit, and on her head was the red wig she'd bought last year on the Internet. Lucille Ball.

Last year the costume was great fun. Last year she was a realtor. Now she was a realtor in a terrifying recession, plus a chambermaid and a short-order cook in a bed-and-breakfast attempt that might fail. On TV this morning there had been a shot of a B-and-B exterior somewhere; for Halloween the owners had put up a funny sign: Dead and Breakfast. So hilarious.

During the past week the weather had gone from sunny and mild to rain and spitting snow to sunny again today. Through it all, the septic-tank project had progressed, the huge tank had been delivered and set in the huge hole and hooked up, and the electrical work was done. Yesterday the septic inspector arrived. The suspense! Bev never dreamed that she might die from the stress of waiting for the result of a septic-tank inspection. When the inspector gave the tank his okay, she nearly fainted with relief. Roger matter-of-factly put a checkmark beside some note on his legal pad.

In other years he had sometimes come with her to see Clem's costume, but this morning he felt he had to stick around

Waterlight because workmen were arriving for the fire-escape project. She figured he'd probably just get in their way.

The bare trees along the road looked bleak. The strip mall's decorations of plastic jack-o'-lanterns looked pathetic, and she couldn't even smile at the laundromat's Halloween sign: Casper Does His Laundry Here! She must rouse herself to match her Lucy costume. The Fabulous Fifties. Past the mall were some dowdy 1950s ranch houses, once desirably modern. She thought: They're like ghosts now.

Then, after some summer cottages and a few old farmhouses, she saw the two signposts side by side, one with a white sign saying in black lettering Beverly Lambert, Realtor, and a lake-blue one whose black letters said Lakes Region Small Engine Sales & Service. Beside them stood Clem and Trulianne, waiting for the bus. Bev waved madly. Clem had his backpack slung over his fleece jacket as usual, but he was holding a pirate's swashbuckling hat. Forty-two-year-old Trulianne didn't wear costumes; she was in her beige corduroy jacket and olive-drab coveralls, her long brown hair twisted into a topknot, safe from machinery. Leon, Clem's father, had grown up tall, dark, and handsome, and Clem continued to take after him, at least in appearance. Clem was almost as tall as his small but sturdy mother. He'd already grown taller than Snowy, who was, as Snowy herself said, shrinking like Alice in Wonderland.

Bev drove into the paved parking lot, past the prefab repair building, and stopped in front of Bide-a-Wee, a blue-trimmed white cottage engulfed over the decades by previous owners' additions, ells and porches and a second story from which dormers peered. The wooden tubs and window boxes were empty, between seasons, between chrysanthemums and evergreens.

When she got out of the car, Clem came sauntering toward her, dangling the hat, unzipping his jacket.

"Ahoy, Lucy," he said.

"Ahoy, kid," she said. "Oops, I mean Captain Kidd."

He wasn't a little boy excitedly showing his grandmother his costume, he was playing it cool, but she knew he was still enjoying costumes as much as she did. Had he inherited the acting gene? For her own pirate costume, Mother had made her a black coat with gold buttons. He opened his jacket and she saw his store-bought costume, a scarlet vest over a white shirt and black pants.

"Wow!" she said.

Trulianne yelled, "The bus is coming!"

At school the kids would go outdoors by grades and parade around the building, and no doubt there'd be other pirates—but Clem would be the best. She couldn't help hugging him, despite the approaching bus with an audience.

He laughed and ran to climb aboard. Bev joined Trulianne, waving. The bus departed.

"Well," Trulianne said. "Another Halloween."

"Thank God for an excuse for a sugar fix. Come in the office and have a devilish treat before you start work." Bev headed back to the car for her shoulder bag and laptop, feeling devilish herself. Trulianne didn't approve of sugar, amongst many other things.

Trulianne said, "So you're Lucy again this year."

"I'm recycling," Bev said. Trulianne ought to approve of that.

They went into the cottage's front hall. When Bev had bought Bide-a-Wee, she had kept for her office the living room, the dining room, the side porch off the dining room, and the half-bath under the stairs in the hall, so that Trulianne's apartment would consist of the kitchen, the family room (with a fireplace), the sewing room, the back porch, a downstairs bedroom, a downstairs bathroom, three upstairs bedrooms, and an upstairs bathroom. Lots of elbow room for Trulianne and Clem. Bev had wondered over the years if a Significant Other might move in. Or might Trulianne even marry, which she hadn't bothered to with Leon? But if there were men (or women) in her life, Trulianne was successfully keeping them secret. Trulianne's life seemed concentrated on repairing engines and taking care of Clem. No sex life? How chaste! How celibate! During her years living apart from Roger, Bev hadn't exactly been a nun.

She opened the door to her office and switched on the lights. Doing so used to be such a pleasure, anticipating the sight of the soothing aquamarine color she'd chosen for the walls and the risky boldness of the upholstery pattern she'd chosen for the furniture, the big flowers in blues and greens and purples. Sometimes it had even made her laugh out loud. But nowadays she felt scared, sickened by the contrast between her high hopes when she decorated the place eight years ago and the feeling of futility now.

The show must go on! Bev pointed to a table's newfangled Keurig coffee machine she'd invested in before money got so tight. She said to Trulianne, “Please, help yourself,” and put the laptop and her shoulder bag on her Pottery Barn mahogany desk. Such a beautiful shoulder bag, woven by Mimi, who had also woven the jade-green curtains on the windows. Now Mimi was scared too. Bev hung her coat on the coat rack, and out of the shoulder bag she took the box of eight Drake’s Devil Dogs she’d grabbed at the supermarket yesterday. Last year she’d brought a box of chocolates to the office in honor of the *I Love Lucy* chocolate-factory episode.

“Here,” Trulianne said, bringing Bev a cup of coffee instead of first pouring one for herself, placing the Lake Winnipesaukee mug on one of the thick coasters woven by Mimi, beside the thistle paperweight that was a present from Snowy’s Scotland trip.

“Thank you.” Sitting down, Bev looked at the Oriental rugs here and in the former dining room she’d furnished with filing cabinets, a fax and a copy machine, and a conference table she’d found at an antiques store. She glanced up.

Trulianne was eyeing the box. “Devil Dogs?”

“A very fifties treat. And why not for breakfast?”

Trulianne suddenly smiled. “My mom has to have a Devil Dog fix occasionally, though not for breakfast, not that I know of.” She returned to the Keurig machine. “For my dad, it’s Wise potato chips, no other brand.”

Bev reached into her paper-napkin supply in a desk drawer, spread out four Devil Dogs invitingly, and unwrapped one for herself. Probably Trulianne had already e-mailed Clem’s maternal grandparents a photo of Pirate Clem this morning.

In Eastbourne on New Hampshire's seacoast, talkative Shirley and taciturn Everett (Trulianne took after her father) lived on Bungalow Court in a little bungalow still filled with Trulianne's three brothers, one who'd never left, two who'd boomeranged home years ago after divorces. Their help with household expenses had allowed Shirley and Everett to retire, Shirley from her job as a desk clerk at a hotel and Everett from his at a roofing company. Retirement! Imagine, rocking on your porch instead of serving B-and-B guests iced tea there. She asked, "Your folks will be here Monday for Clem's birthday party?" and bit into the Devil Dog; all at once, in her mind, Puddles blurted some typically phallic wisecrack about this. She added, "They'll bring the cake?" Shirley always baked Clem's birthday cake, ever since his first birthday, which Bev hadn't known about. Eleven years ago on Monday, Trulianne had gone with Shirley to the Eastbourne hospital instead of to her job as an auto mechanic. Against Trulianne's orders, Shirley had phoned Leon, who arrived in the nick of time for Clem's birth. But Bev hadn't known Clem existed—or Trulianne and the entire Hughes family—until two years later. She and Roger had missed two whole years of their first grandchild's life.

Trulianne said, "Yes, Mom's bringing the cake." She sipped her coffee but she didn't accept a Devil Dog and she didn't sit down in a client's chair or on the sofa.

Or at the other desks in the room, at which her agents used to sit. They had given up by now, even Lorraine Fitch, who had been a hotshot real-estate salesperson at Plumley Real Estate when Bev joined that group. When Bev had opened this office, Lorraine had come with her. Lorraine was seventy-seven now; some real-estate people went on forever, and Bev had expected Lorraine to be this type despite Lorraine's having had an angioplasty a few years ago, but the recession convinced Lorraine to quit after Labor Day. She told Bev, "I'll be back when my savings run out," and then said what people were apt to say about retirement, "Now it's time to stop and smell the roses." Bev, knowing Lorraine's sales history and her Depression-era frugality, was sure that, recession or no recession, she'd saved enough to keep smelling the roses until she was pushing up daisies.

"The birthday-supper menu," Bev said. "Maybe this year it should include Devil Dogs and Wise potato chips. Are you sure you don't want me to make my famous meat loaf?"

Trulianne said, "I have time on my hands too. So this year I can make the meal." She plunked down her mug on the Keurig table. "But today there's Jim Milford's snowmobile he wants ready for the first snowflake." The sudden smile again, and as she left she snagged a Devil Dog off Bev's desk and closed the office door.

Wondering, Bev went to the front window and watched Trulianne cross the yard to her workshop. Had this smile been because of some money coming in from work on the snowmobile or because of Jim Milford himself? He was the manager of the Gunthwaite Hardware Store, fiftyish, recently divorced—

A car with New York license plates turned in at the signs and drove across the yard to park beside Bev's car. A customer! From New York! Bev hastened back to her desk, whisked off her wig, crammed it and the Devil Dogs into a drawer, hauled a notepad out of another, found her silver-rimmed reading glasses in her shoulder bag, opened the laptop, and tried to look busy and prosperous.

Whoever was in the car was dawdling. Bev waited. Finally she heard the front door open. Then there was a little tap on the office door.

Bev made her voice confident. "Please, do come in."

The door was opened by Pauline, the older of Roger's two pretty sisters, age sixty-seven, small and buxom.

Bev stood up. "Pauline?"

Pauline remained in the doorway. Her dark brown hair's pixie cut looked crushed, and instead of a usual carefully chosen outfit she wore a slapdash jacket over a sweatshirt and jeans. She was wearing black-rimmed glasses instead of her contact lenses—and she wasn't wearing any makeup. Not even lipstick! Pauline lived with her husband in upstate New York. Had Roger forgotten to mention that Pauline and Greg were coming for a visit? But why come to the office instead of directly to Waterlight? They had never been to the office before.

Bev stepped out from behind her desk. "Pauline. Are you all right?"

Pauline said, "I burned down our house. It was an accident, but Greg has kicked me out. He told me to go live with Roger."

## 4. Bev

"WHAT?" BEV SAID.

"You heard me," Pauline said.

"Your house?"

Pauline surveyed the office. "This isn't what I pictured. So much floral stuff. It looks more like a hotel."

"A hotel?"

"And now you and Roger are running a hotel in your home."

Bev corrected, "A bed-and-breakfast."

"Breakfast," Pauline said. "Is that one of those one-cup things?" She began walking stiffly toward the Keurig. Then she was keeling over backward.

Bev rushed to grab her, drag her onto the sofa, stuff a floral pillow under her head.

Pauline said, "I drove all night."

Bev pressed the power button on the coffee machine, thought of raiding Trulianne's kitchen for something more healthy but instead took a Devil Dog out of her desk, unwrapped it, snatched a napkin, and hurried to Pauline, who was struggling to sit up. "Eat this."

"Dandy," Pauline said, adjusting her glasses.

"Yes," Bev agreed, removing her own glasses. "Yes, Devil Dogs are dandy—your house, it *burned down*?"

"Dandy! You know, Dandelion, my canary, he's in my car."

Bev had forgotten Dandy. "I can't remember how you like your coffee."

"Right now, black."

"Black," Bev repeated. "Dandy." When, she wondered distractedly, had she and Roger paid a visit after Pauline and Greg moved back to Greg's hometown of Wartling, New York, from Atlanta, Georgia? Four years ago? Yes, and there had been a bird in a cage in the living room of the nice old Dutch Colonial.

Earlier, Pauline and Greg had come to the renewal-of-vows ceremony at Waterlight, and, more recently, two summers ago, they'd stopped by on their way to a week's vacation in Old Orchard Beach, Maine, with no bird accompanying them on either occasion, but hadn't there been a mention of a neighbor bird-sitting? Bev brought her a mug. "Drink this, then I'll take you and Dandy to Waterlight." What, she thought, will Roger say and do?

Pauline sipped, swallowed, bit into the Devil Dog, swallowed, and hugged her jacket around her. "I wasn't scared last night until he turned the lights off."

"Who? Greg?"

"We're living in a motel. He had his say and turned off the light switch and left. I heard his van drive off."

Bev sat down beside Pauline. Greg had made some sort of electrical statement, leaving Pauline in the dark. Bev had always thought him an extremely useful husband. Not only was he an electrician, but he also had a plumber's license; he preferred electrical jobs but if necessary he'd go under a sink or into a toilet. A professional! (Roger had never been useful except with cars.) Greg was semiretired now after a coronary bypass operation, after years of working at a cousin's electrical supply store in Atlanta. Pauline, who, when their three children were all in school, had gone to work as a cashier at an Atlanta supermarket, now filled in at one in Wartling. Roger laughed about Greg's getting the urge to return to the winters of Wartling when his mother died and he inherited the family home, but Bev thought Roger understood as well as she did how your hometown could tug you. Oh, God. The family home. The house that Pauline had burned down was the family home!

Pauline finished the Devil Dog and looked surprised. "You know, I don't think I've had one of these since high school. My kids went for Twinkies." Then she said, "The dark, it was like being blind. I felt around for the beds and the TV and tripped over a luggage rack and got to the light switch. He hadn't locked me and Dandy in. He wanted us to leave, not stay. So I repacked my suitcase and took Dandy out to the car and came straight here. Well, I stopped for gas. He didn't take away my credit card. And well, I did get kind of lost, not paying enough attention."

"Pauline. Your house burned down?"

"It was the dryer. I was drying a laundry load. He says it's because I forgot to clean the lint trap, but I *had*, so it must've been something else, something that he didn't clean, the hose to the outdoors you're supposed to clean and nobody does. If it's not me, if it's him, then his reputation as an electrician—" Pauline swallowed a last gulp of coffee and handed the mug to Bev.

Bev stood up, looking at Pauline, who must still be in shock, doubly in shock, the fire and then Greg's reaction. He had expelled her from their home. Was that possible, was it even legal? And anyway, no matter how angry he was, how could he do that to his wife? He and Pauline had been married as long as she and Roger had, without any years of separation. Pauline had once repeated a comment that the comedian Elayne Boosler had made on TV; Pauline had said, "'They've been married so long they're on their second bottle of Tabasco.' That's us." Bev wanted to pummel her with questions—where were you when the fire started, were you in the house, how did you rescue Dandy and get out, why didn't you phone us—and what about insurance? She said, "Let's go to Waterlight." She thought: How can I handle this on top of everything else?

Pauline rose, seeming steadier now.

Bev donned her jacket and her shoulder bag, collected her laptop, and as they went outdoors Pauline headed for her car, a Toyota, saying, "I'll meet you at Waterlight."

"You'd better come in my car."

"I'm all right now."

"You haven't had any sleep, Pauline. We'll go together in my car." Bev would have to phone Trulianne to explain the New York car parked overnight at Bide-a-Wee.

"I'll get Dandy," Pauline said. On the backseat of her car, Dandy's shrouded cage was wearing a seat belt. To Bev's ears, under the cloth Dandy seemed to be muttering sullenly. The car smelled of birdseed. Pauline removed the cloth and hoisted the cage out, telling him, "It's okay, we're almost home."

Oh, my God. Home?

Also on Pauline's backseat was one lone suitcase, obviously brand-new. Lifting it out, Bev pictured Waterlight burned flat, her possessions gone, and she herself almost keeled over. Poor Pauline! But—*home*? Where would they put Pauline, even temporarily? The bedrooms that weren't in the midst of bathroom-building were empty for the moment, but they were meant for paying guests. When Pauline and Greg had come to the renewal-of-vows ceremony, they'd stayed in the suite. Impossible now for Pauline to stay there. Put Pauline on the sofa bed that was crammed into the master bedroom? Master. Roger. Roger's sister. Bev lugged the suitcase to join Dandy on the backseat of the Subaru. Pauline's worldly goods.

Bev asked, "Do you need to stop and get some food for him?"

"It's in the suitcase." Pauline pointed at the workshop. "That's your grandson's mother's place?"

"Yes. Today she's readying a snowmobile for winter."

"Winter."

They got into the car, and Bev drove out of the parking lot onto North Road trying to remember where Pauline and Greg's children lived. A son in California? A daughter in Georgia and the other son where? All too far away to help immediately, but eventually shouldn't they help either by effecting a reconciliation or by taking their mother in?

Pauline asked, "Could you detour to the Mill Street area?"

Bev glanced at her, more questions teeming, but she made herself only say, "Of course."

Into downtown Gunthwaite they went, along State Avenue to Trask's, the big brick building now a conference center but previously the factory where Pauline and Roger's father had worked. Also Snowy's father. Bev turned onto Mill Street. Some of the old mill houses in this neighborhood had been tidied up, some were being fixed up, and she had sold several over the years. Those years when she was actually selling. She braked in front of the house in which Pauline and Roger and their parents and siblings, Joe, Claire, and Skip, had lived. It had been painted gray then. If she were naming the color (and she'd studied zillions of paint chips in her avocation as painter) she would've called it "Factory-Smoke Gray." Later owners had painted it bright blue with yellow trim.

Perhaps the yellow trim was what caused Dandy to start trilling.

"Yes," Pauline told him over her shoulder, "this is where I grew up." To Bev she said, "Could you drive past Uncle André's store?"

"It isn't a store anymore."

"I know, I know."

Bev drove to the building that had once been Lambert's Market, the neighborhood grocery store, and then had been converted into an odd-looking house, the old plate-glass windows filled in with siding around regular windows.

Pauline told Dandy, "This is my uncle's store, where I met Greg. He and a couple of friends drove from Wartling through New Hampshire to see the Lakes Region on their way to the ocean in Maine, Old Orchard Beach. They were looking for a grocery store to buy cigarettes and beer, and they spotted Uncle André's. I was working that afternoon. I was seventeen. All of us Lambert kids, we worked for Uncle André at one time or another. I guessed the guys were underage for beer—you had to be twenty-one—but I sold them the beer. Hell, *I* was underage. Those were the days. Later I learned Greg was nineteen. They were using his car for their jaunt. Anyway, the next weekend I was working here again and he showed up alone. He invited me to go swimming at Old Orchard." She gave a shrug and a laugh.

The call of the ocean. Bev remembered that Leon had met Trulianne because he had a hankering to see the ocean and had driven to Eastbourne, where his pickup truck had broken down and been taken to the garage where she was a mechanic.

Pauline said, "Okay. Enough."

Bev drove a little over the speed limit down side streets to reach a main road that led to Lakeside Road. She had known the Lamberts ever since she and Roger started dating in high school, but how well did she really know them outside family rituals, how well did she know Pauline? Time for Roger to take over!

She turned at the inn sign and mailbox. When she steered down the circular driveway she saw a pickup and a van parked in front of Waterlight and three men standing there conferring with Roger and his clipboard—or, from their body language, trying to pry loose from him to get on with their work. The fire escape. Escaping fire.

She parked behind the van and stepped out, calling, "Roger! We have a surprise guest!"

The men melted away toward the back of the house. A quizzical expression on his face, Roger walked to the car, clicking his ballpoint. Pauline remained in the passenger seat, and the expression on her face made Bev fear she was going to faint again.

So Bev said, "It's Pauline, Roger. Something awful has happened."

Pauline opened the passenger door, pulling herself upright.

Bev said, "Their house burned down."

"You're shitting me," Roger said.

Bev said, "She'll stay with us for a while."

"Where's Greg?" he asked.

Pauline said, "He kicked me out. He told me to go live with you."

"Huh?"

Pauline moved slowly toward her big brother. Roger put his arms around her.

Her head against his chest, Pauline said, "I could help with the B-and-B," and began to cry.

Over her head, Roger looked at Bev. He didn't smile, he didn't wink, but Bev knew exactly what he was thinking: It's an ill wind that blows nobody any good. She'll be free help!

# Chapter Two

# 1. Snowy

On the morning of Wednesday, November 5, Snowy didn't do her scoliosis yoga routine, she didn't take her usual walk through the village (walking the route she used to run), and she and Tom postponed their showers. At 5:30 she was sitting beside him at the trestle table in their apartment's kitchen area, both still in bathrobes, he in his Royal Stewart flannel fleece-lined bathrobe, she in her pink flannel version. She was clutching her rooster-decorated coffee mug and staring with him at the TV in the living-room area, still not daring to start cheering.

"It's true," said Tom, looking tired, frazzled, his white hair uncombed—and also his white beard (she'd never got used to his combing his face as well as his hair). He set down his coffee mug, a present from Puddles after Snowy's grandson was born; the old-man decoration announced, "I'm sleeping with a grandmother!" He took off his rimless trifocals, put them back on, and stared at the TV screen again.

Snowy repeated, "It's true." During the night they'd kept waking up to listen to the election returns on the bedside radio. Now on the morning TV news it was definite. Definitely definite. A great weight seemed to lift off her and she felt suddenly giddy with relief. Sunrise wouldn't come for an hour yet, but she felt that it was bursting over the horizon.

The phone rang. She jumped up, saw Dudley's caller ID, and grabbed the receiver.

Dudley shouted, "D. J. won! And Obama!"

"They won!" she cheered. "They won!"

"And Jeanne Shaheen!"

Their New Hampshire former governor! And now their first New Hampshire woman in the Senate! Snowy said, "All New Hampshire Democrats won! Our Republican state! Oh, Dudley, remember our mock presidential election in high school, Eisenhower and Adlai Stevenson?"

"You and I and Bev were just about the only Democrats in the class!"

She asked, "You've phoned D. J. and Ruhamah? Did they come home or did they stay at the Holiday Inn?"

"They stayed, too tired to drive home. Victory! With the—what's the word I want, the something-or-other the polls predicted?"

"The margin?"

"That's it. I've phoned D. J. and told him he's destined to be Speaker of the House!"

"I'll phone them now. How is Al?" To give D. J. and Ruhamah freedom during the election-returns gathering at D. J.'s office in Concord, Al had spent the night with his other grandparents, Dudley and Charlene. Al's birth had introduced Snowy to a new emotion: grandparent-jealousy. However, she was still working full-time, while Dudley and Charl were retired and used to babysitting their umpteen other grandchildren, so it made sense for them to take care of Al more often than she did. But still . . .

"He's doing fine," Dudley said. "Charl is tending to his breakfast, and he sends his love."

Breakfast meant Ruhamah's breast-pump supply, which Ruhamah would freeze in small bags and bring to them in a cooler when she and D. J. dropped Al off. Snowy said, "Give him my love." Such a fierce protective love, she thought, the same as the love that had surged through her for baby Ruhamah but intensified by age, by knowing how much could befall a baby, a child, a human being.

"Will do," Dudley said. "I'll read the newspaper headlines to him! Remember being the only Democrats? I'll tell him that. Good-bye!"

"Bye," she said, and hung up, fighting jealousy. Well, next time she was babysitting Al, instead of reciting *A Child's Garden of Verses* and other children's poems, she would introduce prose, not newspaper headlines but a children's book. She would read *Stuart Little* to him, her first E. B. White book, which in elementary school her second-grade teacher had read to the class. Why not for a baby nearly three months old! Or had Dudley, who had been in that class, already done this?

Tom stood up from the table. "Everything okay?"

"Rejoicing. I'll phone Ruhamah." She glanced at the kitchen's rooster clock. "Dudley got through but their phones may be busy even this early."

"I'll take my shower. I may sing in it."

Ruhamah's cell phone was indeed busy, so Snowy tried D. J.'s but it was also. Rejoicing.

And she had to get going; she had to open the store at 7 a.m. She heard Tom in the shower begin to sing "We Shall Overcome," and she laughed.

No time to make a celebratory breakfast. Near the toaster she set out Tom's English muffin, Promise margarine, and marmalade, and then she spooned her fat-free yogurt out of its carton into a bowl, the morning routine seeming fresh and revived by—relief. She glanced over her shoulder at the TV. Yes, it was true.

Domesticity, she thought, returning to the fridge, taking out a jug of maple syrup and pouring a dollop over the yogurt for a mini-celebration. She and Tom, amused, had found that married life after all these years of living together actually increased intimacy. Had she feared that a wedding, a formal announcement of their love, would turn them into a dull couple who didn't talk to each other in restaurants? Had he feared a prison? Around her in the apartment were the same items they'd combined earlier, such as her mother's rooster collection (ceramic and otherwise, to which she was adding), the rug her grandmother had braided, Tom's father's World War II souvenirs from the Philippines, and the record-player-radio cabinet Tom had made in high-school shop, but now they seemed even more intertwined.

A New Hampshire weather report came on the TV. The thermometer outside the kitchen window registered 43°. The report told her that today would be hazy, warm, up into the lower 60s. In November. Climate change. Could there be hope after this election?

The kitchen wall phone rang. Snowy put her bowl down, saw that it was Ruhamah, and seized the receiver, saying, "Isn't this wonderful, congratulations!"

Ruhamah's distinctive voice, a chortle, was full-throttle. "In a way it's even more exciting than two years ago, it's a confirmation, an affirmation, but it's more scary too. Snowy, I've just had a call from Donna to congratulate us but also asking if you might be able to go up to see her today. She didn't say what it's about, I assume it's that problem with the milk delivery again, but what with all that's happening here I didn't quiz her, you know how she is and she seemed really agitated. So why don't you call Rita about filling in while you tend to Donna?"

Oh, damn, Snowy thought. But she said, "Don't worry, I'll handle it."

"Thanks, keep me posted, see you tomorrow, bye!"

Donna Welch was the manager of the Thetford General Store, which they'd bought in 2005, the second store in their little three-store empire. Donna had a tendency to go to pieces under pressure, a trait that Snowy knew she herself possessed, alas. But Donna was a very nice woman, fifty-two years old, never married, and a Thetford local, a fixture; the town was fond of her. Snowy sighed. Phoning Rita might be touchy because Rita had voted for John McCain, mostly because she admired Republican vice-presidential candidate Sarah Palin's attitude and clothes. Rita Beaupre Henderson Barlow lived in the farmhouse that Snowy and Alan had bought in 1985 along with the store when they moved to Woodcombe. After Alan's suicide and the discovery of the store's near-bankruptcy, Snowy had sold Hurricane Farm to Frank Barlow, before his marriage to Rita. Now widowed and well-off, Rita worked part-time at the store and ran it alone when necessary, preferring the latter.

Snowy took a deep breath and tapped Rita's number.

"Hi," Rita said. "I bet you're turning cartwheels about Obama."

They'd been partners on the Gunthwaite High School cheerleading squad. Snowy said, "It's a busy morning, isn't it. Ruhamah had a—"

"Congratulations to her and D. J. I told you I was going to split my ticket, vote for D. J., and I did."

"Thank you, Rita. Ruhamah had a call from Donna, so I should go to Thetford sometime today. Is there a chance you could take care of the store for a couple of hours?"

Rita said, "Well . . . "

But Snowy could tell from her tone she'd be delighted to get out of the house and into post-election rehashing at the store. "It'd be a tremendous help, Rita."

"I'll be there around eight."

"Thank you!" Hanging up, Snowy next phoned Donna, picturing her, tall and slender with a pleasant unadorned face, in the Thetford house in which she'd lived all her life, alone since her parents died. "Hi, Donna, Ruhamah phoned me, and I'll be up at your store about eight-thirty. Is the problem the milk delivery?"

Donna's clear telephone voice had been acquired, Snowy assumed, during the office work she'd done in a couple of Lakes Region businesses before going to work for the married couple who had previously owned the Thetford General Store. She usually sounded calmer than she was apt to be, but today she did sound very rattled. "No, no, I'm sorry to bother you but, well, there's something to discuss."

Tom emerged from the bathroom in his bathrobe, looking steamy. "It's all yours."

Snowy said to Donna, "Okay. I'll see you soon."

In the shower, she sang labor songs from Pete Seeger records, "Union Maid" and "We Shall Not Be Moved" and "John Henry." She came out of the bathroom to find Tom dressed and watching TV, his English muffin toasted but uneaten.

He said, "I think I'm going to have to keep checking the news all day. To keep making sure."

"Yes."

In their bedroom she pulled on underwear, jeans, and, diplomatically, a Thetford instead of a Woodcombe General Store sweatshirt. Then she went into the spare bedroom she had turned into her office. Bookcases; filing cabinets; a faded aqua butterfly chair she'd spotted in an antiques store and bought because it reminded her of the orange butterfly chair she'd had at Bennington. She opened the laptop on the computer desk beside the old mahogany veneer desk. An e-mail had arrived from Harriet, her Bennington roommate, who lived in Manhattan and had bought Bev's childhood home for a New Hampshire country retreat. Harriet wrote, "Not Hillary, but hooray! And congratulations to Ruhamah and D. J.!"

Snowy typed a quick reply, "We'll celebrate when you're up here at Thanksgiving," and hurried back to the kitchen. She started to lift her blue fleece jacket off a hook; the phone rang. She told Tom, "Bev," and into the phone she said, "Hi, there."

"They won!" Bev exclaimed. "D. J. and Obama!"

Snowy said, "We're stunned."

"God, it's so exhilarating to have some *good* news for a change. This isn't the milestone that Hillary would've been, but what a milestone it is!"

Snowy hesitated, then asked, "How is Pauline doing? Which room did you put her in?"

"Leon's old room, aka the Grebe Room. She's still in shock, I think. She's clinging to Roger. She came with us to Clem's birthday party. She wanted to bring Dandy, but Roger convinced her the weather was too cold so she left him in her room, and maybe that's progress."

"Has her husband phoned? Has she phoned him?"

"Silence, as far as I know. Roger just keeps saying to give them time. I keep saying that if we don't call Greg, we must at least phone their children. He says probably Greg has notified the kids about the fire and probably Pauline has phoned the kids to tell them about that, if not about Greg's kicking her out. She could feed them a story about how she came here to help us during the fire's aftermath, the insurance and all. Roger says not to interfere. She's gone clothes-shopping, so I guess she assumes—or hopes—Greg will pay when he gets the credit-card statement. Anyway! Give Ruhamah and D. J. congratulations from Roger and me. Bye!"

"Bye." Snowy hung up, and the phone rang again. She told Tom, "Puddles," picturing her in Maine, in the old saltwater farm belonging to generations of her husband's family, Puddles looking both fragile and stalwart and getting ready to start a stint at the Long Harbor clinic, where she worked three mornings a week; she also coached the Long Harbor High School cheerleaders several afternoons.

Puddles yelled, "Holy shit, Obama won! And D. J. won again!"

"We can't believe it yet."

"And all those New Hampshire Democrats! What happened to the Granite State's Grand-Old-Party Republicans?"

"Massachusetts folks invaded us."

"Good for the Massholes! Okay, Snowy, D. J.'s election is over so that's off your to-do list, so when are you and Tom finally going to get away for your honeymoon? You two are slower than cold molasses!"

Snowy looked at Tom sipping coffee and thought of the day's work enclosing them, the responsibilities, the routine resumed. "I don't know, Puddles."

## 2. Snowy

After she opened the store and customers began coming in, it was easy to tell the Democrats from the Republicans if you didn't already know, which she pretty much did. At the cash register Snowy sold newspapers to some jubilant townsfolk; at the lunch counter she poured coffee in which dejected townsfolk could drown their sorrows. One-hundred-year-old Gladys Stanton was jubilant but looking to the future. Last February, on the day of the New Hampshire Primary, Gladys had held a Hillary sign outside the town hall, as had Snowy and Tom. In June, when Obama got the Democratic nomination, Gladys had come in to the store and declared to Snowy, "Hope springs eternal. I'm going to defy the odds and live to see a woman president of the United States." Today she said, "I'm happy I've lived long enough to see this, and damnit, I'm still determined to live to see a woman president." Someone at the lunch counter, overhearing Gladys, snorted.

On the dot of 8 a.m., Rita arrived, her usual vivid self, black hair bouffant, eye shadow lilac. Snowy felt pale, exhausted from exercising customer-tact.

"Okay," Rita said, unbuttoning her red leather jacket that matched her lipstick, "I'm here, you can leave. What's up with Donna?"

"Oh, this and that." Snowy headed for the broom closet and her own jacket hanging there.

Rita said, "It's going to be warm today, she could go skinny-dipping."

Donna, Snowy thought, would never live down her skinny-dipping adventure of this past summer. Misadventure. "Thank you, Rita, for coming. I'll be back as soon as I can."

"Take your time," said Rita.

Snowy waved good-bye to customers and walked up the street to the barn. Yes, today would be warm, but not so warm as a day last summer when, as Donna had told her, into the Thetford General Store strolled a man whom Donna hadn't seen since they were high-school kids working together one summer at Peggy Ann's, Donna a waitress, Brian a busboy. Their summer romance didn't last into the school year because Brian and his family moved away—to Texas! All these years later he'd reappeared in Thetford on a trip east. He was an antiques dealer, had been scouting and buying in New England, and was staying a couple of nights in a motel in the area before heading back to Austin. And he was single, long-divorced. He'd invited Donna to dinner at Peggy Ann's, for old times' sake, and after dinner for more old times' sake they went on in his car to the Thetford Lake beach where they'd sometimes gone swimming at night after work. Outside the air-conditioning of the car, the evening was hot. They didn't have bathing suits. Oh, what the hell! They got undressed—and "fooled around," as Donna demurely put it. They tossed their clothes into the car and dashed into the lake. And swam. And fooled around. When they returned to the car they found it locked. Panic for Donna. Oh, God! Oh, my God, how? Had his car keys in his pants pocket inadvertently locked it? Brian resourcefully located a suitable rock and broke a window. The car alarm started shrieking. Someone at a cottage down the shore phoned the police. And the next morning Thetford and all its environs knew.

And Brian returned to the Lone Star State.

The pickup truck belonging to David, Tom's son, wasn't yet in the barn's driveway, but he would soon be driving here from his house on Crescent Street, where he lived with wife

Lavender and their daughters, to start the day's work with Tom. Before she got into her car, she opened the barn's smaller door and stuck her head in. Tom looked up from his rolltop desk.

She called, "It's true!"

"It's true!"

"I'm off to Thetford now."

"Drive carefully."

Along Main Street she drove, the campaign signs in front yards looking suddenly dated—or did they look innocent, not yet knowing the outcome? Thank God this would also be the end of the tough Republican TV ads against D. J., at least for the next two years.

Then the road climbed up out of the valley, the haze smudging the mountain views. Tom had once commented, "Woodcombe is an island. In its way." However, Woodcombe was land-locked. *Land-locked.* That word was the title of a poem by Celia Thaxter who in the 1800s had written it inland, homesick for the Isles of Shoals, the islands Snowy used to see on the horizon from the seacoast house in Pevensay in which she and Alan had lived before moving to Woodcombe and becoming land-locked, living inland. And "Inland" was the title of a poem by Edna St. Vincent Millay on the subject. She herself, Henrietta Snow, had certainly written about this. But since the publication of her *Selected Poems* last year, she had mostly been writing about Maine's coast, especially since she and Tom had spent two weeks there last April. Puddles's husband, Blivit, had found them a cottage on Quarry Island off the coast of his hometown, Long Harbor, after she had phoned Puddles and, desperate, asked about any cottages to rent on the island. Blivit had come up with Cotter Cottage, owned by his eighty-seven-year-old Aunt Izzy's granddaughter's husband's great-aunt, Mildred Cotter, who had been born and brought up on a Quarry Island farm and then had worked as a secretary at a Portland law firm until she retired to this island cottage she'd bought. But a year ago at age eighty-eight, Mildred had had a fall, had broken her right leg and ended up in a rehabilitation place in Portland. Thus Snowy and Tom could rent the cottage. He hadn't wanted to go but she had forged ahead, hoping the island would help lift the depression that had descended after his knee replacements. Cotter Cottage had turned out to be a humdrum old ranch house in need of upkeep, but it was right smack on the ocean, and the change of scenery had indeed helped him. On their way home they'd stopped at the nursing home to thank Mildred, who was longing for the sea. Of course. As Celia Thaxter had written:

O happy river, could I follow thee!<br>
O yearning heart, that never can be still!<br>
O wistful eyes, that watch the steadfast hill,<br>
Longing for level line of solemn sea!

Through the stark trees Snowy glanced at Lower Lake, misty, pretty, but not the sea. Ye gods, she and Tom *must* get away to Maine.

Reaching the highway and heading north, she saw the full parking lot of Peggy Ann's Place, a popular restaurant busy with breakfast and probably teeming with the same assortment of reactions that had been displayed at the store. Maybe she and Tom could come here after work for a celebratory dinner of Peggy Ann's renowned baked ham.

She punched on the radio, then admonished herself, "They *did* win!" and switched it off. She buzzed down her window.

Soon Snowy swung onto Thetford Road. Ahead the Paugus River went lolloping between wooded banks, under the covered bridge that always caught the attention of tourists on the highway and tempted them to make this picturesque detour. Many tourists did. The steady tourist trade as well as the loyal locals had convinced Ruhamah to buy the Thetford General Store when the owners acknowledged they were getting too old and worn out to continue and had put it up for sale. Snowy thought: Am I getting too old and worn out?

Thetford took good care of its Paugus River Bridge, which had been built in 1870. Most recently the town had voted extra money for work to be done on its underpinnings, and the brown wooden walls had been freshly stained. So it looked more trustworthy than some covered bridges she'd seen and experienced, but nevertheless she always held her breath as she slowed the car way down and entered its shadowy interior, bumping from macadam onto the board floor. There were several covered-bridge traditions, such as kissing or making a wish. She always fervently wished the bridge would not collapse.

When she emerged on the other side, she exhaled.

O happy river, could I follow thee!

She had grown up with a river across the street from her parents' house, so she took an interest in the houses built along this river, those with a backyard boat now covered with plastic for the winter, other houses just looking residential, including Donna's family home. She and Donna certainly didn't have a long commute; they both could do that old-fashioned thing, walk to work.

The river spread out behind a dam, then in a waterfall dropped into Main Street beside the general store and disappeared under a road bridge, continuing behind Main Street, past the new fire station built on the site of the old lumber mill, past the white clapboard town hall, the little stone library, the white clapboard post office, the white clapboard church, and the mill owner's pale-yellow gabled mansion now divided into apartments.

Only one car was parked in the white clapboard store's small parking lot. Snowy parked and got out slowly, stretching her back. The day was now warm enough not to need a jacket. She removed hers and put it in the car, thinking of Donna's and Brian's clothes. Lifting her shoulder bag off the passenger seat, she walked past the single gas pump and went indoors.

This store was smaller than Woodcombe's and simply a store, without a lunch counter and tables, so Donna could handle it on her own, calling in another local woman to help or take over when necessary. After Snowy and Ruhamah had bought the store, they'd suggested Donna add touches of her own to the place. Donna had hung home-dried flowers from the rafters, silvery explosions of everlastings, and she'd created a little gardening corner in spring and summer on the shelves;

its items included packets of seeds and pairs of cute gloves, but now they were replaced by groceries again until next spring.

At the cash register, Donna caught Snowy's eye but kept on listening to a woman customer who, paying for a cabbage, a box of cake mix, and a tube of toothpaste, was saying, "I can't wait to see what Michelle Obama decides to wear to the inauguration, she wears clothes so well." The woman saw Snowy and exclaimed, "Speaking of clothes, you two are twins!"

Donna was also wearing jeans and a Thetford General Store sweatshirt. But since Donna was at least ten inches taller than Snowy, she wore them better. Today her light brown ponytail was pulled up, smooshed flat, and bobby-pinned against the back of her head. "Hi, Snowy," Donna said, bagging the purchases. To the woman she said, "I'll put aside that loaf of French bread when the bread comes in."

"Thank you." The woman left.

Donna patted the high stool behind the checkout counter and said to Snowy, "Why don't you sit here."

Snowy walked around the counter, dumped her shoulder bag beneath it, and sat.

Donna said, "I gave Ruhamah my congratulations, to her and D. J."

"She told me. Thank you, Donna."

Donna turned and gazed out the front window at Main Street.

Snowy did too.

Donna began to tremble. She said, "I'm going to move to Austin, Texas."

Snowy stood up, sat down again.

"I promise," Donna said, holding on to the counter, steadying herself, "I promise I won't leave you in the lurch. I told Brian I wouldn't marry him until you find someone to take my place."

"Brian?"

"He hasn't been back since this summer but there's the telephone and e-mail and, well, old-fashioned mail." Donna paused, then quavered, "Love letters."

"*Texas?*"

Out the window, a pickup truck pulled alongside the gas pump. A guy got out, unhooked the gas nozzle and began pumping.

Donna said, "Last spring Cheryl, one of my friends, decided not to have her birthday party at a restaurant around here, Peggy Ann's or anywhere. She wanted a fancy dinner and some dancing in Manchester, all the way to Manchester, and she invited me to come along with her and her husband and three other couples, all of us friends, in two cars. Is your back hurting? You look like it's hurting."

"It's fine."

"I'm used to being the extra," Donna said, "and I find it interesting. I'm used to being on my own. But when they got up to dance, the girls—women—didn't want to leave their pocketbooks on their chairs even if I was guarding the table, so they piled their pocketbooks on my lap and I sat there and held the pocketbooks and watched my friends dancing with their husbands."

The guy hung up the nozzle and headed for the store to pay.

"So when Brian proposed in a letter," Donna said, "I remembered the dancing and said yes, even if it meant leaving Thetford." Then she went to pieces. She cried, "Leaving Thetford! Selling my house! I won't leave until you find someone, but am I crazy, at my age—you didn't marry Tom until now but you'd lived with Tom all those years and you didn't move away—to *Texas*—"

Snowy stood up again and this time put her arms around her.

The guy froze in the doorway, looking nonplussed.

Snowy told him, "Donna has some happy news for our customers."

## 3. Bev

LINGERIE, BEV THOUGHT FURIOUSLY, STANDING IN THE LAUNDRY room off Waterlight's kitchen and filling the sink with cold water. She hadn't actually hand-washed her underwear in decades; she used the hand-wash cycle of the washing machine. But now here she was pouring in some Tide and plunging three days' worth of her nylon "lingerie" into the suds, all because of a clogged filter in the washing machine so no water would come in, because of this and an absent plumber and other plumbers too busy to rescue her right now. How primitive! What next, washing clothes in the lake, beating them against a rock?

Don't be so nerved-up, she told herself. Pauline had taken a load to the laundromat.

Out the window the late afternoon seemed braced for the holiday. Today was the day before Thanksgiving, when almost everyone in America was traveling somewhere to get to family, including Joel, her usual faithful plumber, who'd left through yesterday's snow and sleet—

She splashed suds, almost soaking her sweater, a dressy white sweater with an embroidered black loon amid green reeds. A "best" sweater. There was a hierarchy in underwear too, your newest down to your rags, and she wanted her best to wear during the holiday weekend. Waterlight's first Thanksgiving as a B-and-B. The new bathrooms had been finished in the nick of time. But only one reservation had been made, and that was made by Dudley and Charl's daughter-in-law Elinor, not by somebody from away who'd seen Roger's ads in *New Hampshire Magazine* and *Yankee* magazine so he would learn the ads were getting results, what he called "market research" or some such asinine term, though with or without encouragement he would be going ahead with a website designer to have the Inn at East Bay's site ready before Christmas. Elinor, wife of Johnny Washburn, Charl and Dudley's oldest child, had phoned to say they needed a guest room this Thanksgiving because their daughter had got married in June and couldn't stay in her old bedroom with its single bed this Thanksgiving when she and her new husband drove up to Gunthwaite from Massachusetts. Roger was pleased that Elinor had asked for the Loon Suite. More expensive! And for three nights, tonight, tomorrow, and Friday.

The guests' names were Lydia and Trent Peterson. They were due any moment, and Bev had put on her loon sweater for them when she changed her clothes after she and Miranda had spent the entire day cleaning the entire downstairs so not a speck of dust would have settled on any surface before the guests arrived. In the suite, Bev had remembered all the nice touches, the hair dryer, the soap, the two gold-foil-wrapped chocolate turkeys on the king-size pillows—

Fiercely she wrung out her bras and dropped them in a plastic dishpan.

The Citigroup bailout had been announced on Monday. The government bailing out a bank! How could it have come to this? And, she had asked Roger, wouldn't everybody be even more unnerved and would never *ever* indulge in the luxury of a winter vacation at a lakeside inn? Roger hadn't answered. Right now he was off at the Home Depot once again on some mission.

When he was planning to start this B-and-B, he'd said that he would be in charge of maintenance and she would be in charge of the guests. He had called her "decorative"! So, plus doing all her other chores, she was supposed to ooze elegant hospitality. She glanced at the full-length mirror left over from the days when this room was also the sewing room. She did not look decorative. The word that leapt to her mind was "haggard." Back in her Connecticut days, when she had played Della in the Ninfield Players' production of *The Gift of the Magi*, she had prayed, "Please God, make him think I'm still pretty." In bed Roger still found her decorative, didn't he? Did he see the Queen of the Junior Prom? Probably he'd forgotten that. But in bed she remembered him playing basketball in the high-school gym, running and swerving as he dribbled the ball, leaping, twisting at the net, scoring. High school. How pathetic! Wasn't it?

"I'm back!" Pauline called from the kitchen and came into the laundry room lugging the clothesbasket piled with folded items.

If only Greg the electrician-plumber had moved into Waterlight instead of Pauline. Then it suddenly struck Bev that the sight of all those dryers at the laundromat might have been traumatic for Pauline.

"Laundromats," Pauline said, plunking the basket on the counter. "They've gone high-tech since the last time I went to one, it's a good thing there was an attendant to show me how."

So Pauline was apparently okay. "Thank you," Bev said, wringing out underpants. "I'll put things away after I finish my unmentionables—"

"And naturally the supermarket was a zoo, the aisles jammed, the checkout lines a mile long."

"I bet." Bev could well imagine this, women in a last-minute rush, punch-drunk from Thanksgiving-dinner preparations, grabbing extra bags of stuffing mix just in case, extra cans of cranberry sauce, as she herself had very often done. This year most of her family members were going to Mimi's for Thanksgiving, Mimi having insisted because Bev would probably be too busy with the inn to make the dinner, but still Bev had needed some last-minute supplies such as Lactaid after Elinor belatedly phoned to say that Lydia, the daughter, was lactose-intolerant. Dropping the underwear into the washing machine and switching the dial to Gentle Spin, she told Pauline, "Thank you for braving the crowds." Ever since moving in, Pauline had made herself extremely useful;

however, Pauline kept pointing this out. Don't snipe, she chided herself. It was bad enough for Pauline to be stranded here, but to be cut off from her family during the holidays must be devastating. Or, she wondered, watching Pauline lift the folded clothes (including Roger's underwear) out of the basket, was it a holiday from the work of having her family come home to be fed a feast? Pauline hadn't mentioned what normally occurred. Was she maybe relieved to be unencumbered, no house, no Thanksgiving responsibilities of her own? Bev hesitated, then blurted, "Your traditions—you haven't said—I don't want to pry but it's Thanksgiving—do your children usually come to your house for Thanksgiving or do you and Greg go to one of their homes? Your grandchildren—"

Pauline interrupted, "Have you ever left the house with a wash load in the dryer?"

"Left the house?"

In a rush Pauline said, "That day was one of my days off from working at the supermarket, and I was in a hurry to get stuff done around the house so I could go do errands and have lunch with a friend. Greg was across town doing the wiring for somebody's new hot-water heater. I took the load out of the washing machine and threw it in the dryer and left. But damnit, I'd checked the lint trap before I turned the dryer on! As I was driving home after a nice long lunch, I got a call. From Greg. Neighbors had phoned him, and he was at our house. The firemen had rescued Dandy. I guess I drove the rest of the way on autopilot."

Bev stared at her. "Pauline, I'm so sorry, I didn't mean to remind you—"

Pauline said, "I hear a car." She bustled out toward the hallway.

Bev transferred her stare to the dryer in this laundry room. The only times she'd left a dryer running weren't deliberate actions, just absentmindedness. Should she tell Roger what Pauline had just told her? No. Let Pauline tell him.

Then she fussed with her sweater in the mirror, smoothed her hair, and followed.

In the front hallway, the door was open and Pauline was on the porch, hurrying down the steps. The white car parked there had Massachusetts license plates and the teardrop shape of one of those hybrid cars. A young woman was stepping out from the passenger seat; a serious parka, long dark hair swinging free from a center part. A young man unfolded himself from behind the steering wheel and stood, looking back up the driveway, bespectacled, rumpled blond curls. He said to Pauline, "That's a fine glacial erratic you have up there."

"A what?" Pauline asked.

Lydia said, "Don't mind him, he means a big rock."

Bev remembered that Elinor had told her Lydia and Trent were both science types and taught at a community college, Lydia biology, Trent geology. She decided it was high time to make an entrance, decoratively or not. She opened the porch's screen door and descended the steps, saying, "Welcome to the Inn at East Bay. I'm Beverly Lambert. How was your trip?"

"Oh," Trent said, looking from Pauline to her, "you're the Bev that Lydia's mom mentioned."

"And this is my sister-in-law Pauline," Bev said. "May we help with your luggage?"

"Thanks," Trent said, "but I can manage," and took two duffel bags out of the back.

The younger generation! At their age, Bev thought, she would've arrived with at least one suitcase, a vanity case, and a garment bag. She held out her right hand to Lydia. "Again, welcome. I've known your grandparents forever."

Lydia laughed and shook her hand. "So Dad told us."

In the hallway, at Roger's big desk, Bev opened the guest book. As Lydia signed it with the ballpoint pen engraved *The Inn at East Bay*, Bev said, "Lydia is a pretty name. It's my mother's mother's name, and if I'd had a third daughter I would have named her Lydia."

Lydia looked up. "What did you name them instead?"

"One is Julia Marie, for my mother and mother-in-law, nicknamed Mimi, and one is Henrietta, for my best friend, and nicknamed Etta."

"Beverly is a pretty name too. Is it for somebody in your family?"

Bev loved to tell stories, but she cut this one short. "A branch of my mother's family came from a town in England, in Yorkshire, named Beverley, spelled with an extra 'e.' Roger and I visited it when we were in England eight years ago on our second honeymoon." She didn't explain that she'd snuck this northern detour into Roger's itinerary of Warwick Castle and Oxford and Blenheim Palace and her choice, Stratford-upon-Avon. Nor did she tell Lydia how she had wished her mother were accompanying her on the tour of that town, not Roger, who had been polite about her ancestral hometown but obviously long-suffering during the sightseeing, even the church called a Gothic masterpiece. He did like the pubs, though.

Lydia marveled, "Second honeymoon! We just had our first."

"On our first," Bev said, "we went to Camden, Maine."

"We went to Prince Edward Island."

Bev said, "Anne of Green Gables! And her red hair! This white hair of mine was once red."

Lydia laughed.

Trent cleared his throat and said to Lydia, "We're supposed to be at your parents' for supper."

Pauline said, "The Loon Suite is all ready."

Thoughtless, Bev rebuked herself, you're thoughtless to be talking about honeymoons in front of Pauline. Bev said, "Please, Pauline, you lead the way."

But Lydia spotted Teddy the moose over the living-room fireplace, so the procession paused as she ran across to gaze up at him with, Bev supposed, a biologist's professional eyes.

Pauline said to Bev, "Do you remember where Greg and I went on our honeymoon?"

Bev made a mad guess. "Old Orchard Beach?"

"Where else?" asked Pauline.

And as Lydia ran back to join them, Bev thought suddenly of the chocolate turkeys waiting in the suite. Milk chocolate. So lactose-intolerant Lydia couldn't enjoy this nice touch.

# 4. Bev

THE NEXT DAY, BEV CHOSE A THANKSGIVING OUTFIT CONSISTING OF a made-by-Mimi shades-of-green woven vest, a white turtleneck jersey, and black jeans. She put Roger in the dark brown vest Mimi had made him, to match his eyes, over a long-sleeved orange-red T-shirt she herself had given him last Thanksgiving; it said Gobble Gobble Gobble. Pauline was wearing a new gold-colored dress. Mimi had invited them for noon, timing dinner between the naps of Jeremy, Etta and Steve's son. Donning parkas, at quarter after eleven they went outdoors into the bright cold morning, Bev carrying her wicker pie basket containing the mince pie from Indulgences.

Down at the dock, ropes on pilings showed that Monday morning Roger and Leon had put in the ice agitator. It was a chilly and windy procedure, one of them on each end of the rope, lowering the metal contraption that would, when freezing began, start churning to keep ice from forming and harming the dock. What with Roger shouting orders and Leon ignoring them (Leon had done the agitator installations by himself before Roger moved in), Bev expected that either father or son or both would fall off the dock into the invigorating waters of Lake Winnipesaukee.

After Roger had moved to Waterlight, he had eventually changed his mind about vehicles. He'd sold his Toyota SUV and plow and bought a pickup truck with a heavier-duty plow. And to her surprise he'd also sold his beloved ancient black Porsche. This summer he'd had the inn's name, address, and phone number painted on the truck's driver's-side door. The narrow backseat would be unsuitable for Pauline, so Bev wasn't surprised when now as they walked toward the garage he announced, "We'll go in the Subaru." And she certainly wasn't surprised when he added, "I'll drive."

She said to Pauline, "You sit up front with him to enjoy the sights of Gunthwaite and Leicester."

Settling herself and her shoulder bag on the backseat, she held the pie basket on her lap and tried to relax as Roger drove off through Gunthwaite, reminiscing with Pauline about childhood Thanksgivings. Although Mimi and Lloyd weren't fans of mince pie, she and Roger were, as were Etta and Steve. She'd be seeing Etta and Steve soon! And little Jeremy! They had driven up from Massachusetts yesterday to spend last night and tonight at Mimi's. She hadn't seen them in ever so long—well, not since she and Roger went down in July to celebrate Jeremy's second birthday.

Her backseat view of Pauline's lengthening pixie cut showed that Pauline's gray roots *really* needed touching up. But Pauline hadn't asked her which salon she went to, so she couldn't suggest it. Closing her eyes, she gave silent Thanksgiving thanks to Pauline—in addition to those she'd said aloud to Pauline—for making Lydia and Trent's breakfast this morning, bacon and lactose-free scrambled eggs, before they went to Elinor and Johnny's house to spend the day. Pauline had replied, "We ought to serve more interesting things than bacon and eggs and toast and muffins and scones. Magazines give me ideas for meals. I'll look for breakfast ideas."

Bev opened her eyes and saw the outskirts of Leicester, where the big-box stores were catching their breath before the Black Friday onslaught. Interrupted by traffic lights, the highway passed Home Depot (Roger's home away from home), Staples, Walmart, and Lowe's (Roger's second home), not to mention Kohl's and Market Basket and Applebee's and Chili's. Then, after a car dealership and a garden-supply store, there were some straggling houses and then ahead a large white farmhouse.

Bev did mental math and leaned forward to tell Pauline, "There's Mimi and Lloyd's. Twenty years ago, when I was working for Plumley Realty, I listed this house and convinced them to invest in it instead of staying in their Leicester apartment." From Connecticut Roger had helped with the purchase; Bev's share of the commission had become a present to Mimi to help her renovate the front rooms for her Weaverbird shop. Bev had hired Leon to do the carpentry. A family project, even if the parents had been living apart.

Pauline said, "An old house. They must've had to put a lot of work into it."

"God, yes," Roger said, flicking his directionals to turn left at Weaverbird's classy white sign, made by Lloyd. "It was built before the Civil War, what did they expect?"

Pauline said, "Greg's folks had let the house go, so we put a lot of work into it."

In the driveway, Roger parked behind Etta's Subaru Forester, which was parked behind Lloyd's truck and Mimi's Weaverbird van. Before she became a shop owner, Mimi had plastered her vehicles with environmental bumper stickers, but since then she'd been discreet with a single bumper sticker at a time. This one said Save It, Don't Pave It. Leon and Miranda weren't here yet. And alas, Dick and Jessica and their little girls wouldn't be here at all, because on Thanksgiving they went to Jessica's family in Connecticut. But they'd be at Waterlight for Christmas!

Getting out of the car, Bev pointed to the heaps of mulch hay in a long rectangle beside the house. She told Pauline, "The barn had already fallen down by the time Mimi and Lloyd bought this place. They cleared it out and turned the site into a gorgeous garden."

Pauline said, "Greg's folks had let their garden go too. I busted my ass."

Bev lifted the pie basket off the backseat and followed Roger and Pauline, Roger leading the way not up the walk to the front door, which was for customers, but along the path around the house to the back door, which Mimi opened before he could knock. Thanksgiving aromas wafted outward from the kitchen, predominantly the dear familiar Bell's Seasoning blend: rosemary, oregano, sage, ginger, marjoram, thyme. Now forty-six, tall and thin, her face sharpening with the years, Mimi was looking more and more like Mother, even though Mother's hair had been short and white, while Mimi's long braid was still light brown.

"Welcome!" Mimi said, but her voice sounded uncertain. "Welcome, Pauline!" Was she worried about celebrating Thanksgiving with a woman whose house had just burned down? She stood back, and they all stepped inside, Roger hugging her, Pauline surveying the kitchen that, Bev always thought, told you right away that arts-and-crafts people lived here, from the stencils of fruits and flowers on the walls to the woven café curtains. This décor continued through the doorway into the dining room, where the table was set with woven place mats.

Around the pie basket, Bev hugged Mimi, feeling how tense she was under her Weaverbird T-shirt. Bev whispered, "Is everything all right?"

Mimi took the basket from her and carried it to the dessert section of the counter, where the mince pie joined a pumpkin pie and what was probably apple. "All under control," she said. "Let me take your jackets—" But she stopped to hover over the huge slow cooker and said, "It's done."

Pauline exclaimed, "You use a Crock-Pot for turkey too! So do I!"

When Thanksgiving was held at Mimi and Lloyd's house, calm Lloyd always cooked the turkey and he did it in the Crock-Pot. Which to Bev was heresy. But the method spared Mimi a lot of work and left the whole oven free for everything else. Bev realized she was hearing a TV from the room Mimi and Lloyd used for a living room, the real living room at the front having become the Weaverbird showroom. That's where Lloyd and Steve would be, watching TV. And Etta must be upstairs tending Jeremy. Bev hung her parka on a peg and asked, "What can I do to help?"

Mimi looked out a window. "Leon and Miranda have arrived. We're all here."

Pauline tossed her new parka over a kitchen chair and set down her shoulder bag. "What needs doing?"

The back door opened. The difference in Leon's and Miranda's ages seemed less obvious now that Leon at forty-two had acquired some gray hairs. Anyway, although Miranda was fifty-four she seemed ageless, with her wire-rimmed glasses halfway down her nose, her brown hair in a ponytail. She had been divorced before Leon moved into her double-wide in Pemberton Park; she had survived breast cancer; her son and daughter and their families were doing well in Seattle. Aside from the agitator project, Bev hadn't seen Leon since he and Clem had invited her and Roger to the dedication ceremony for Clem's elementary school's sap house that Leon had just finished building. She had attended; Roger had been busy, and she'd been glad because when the school principal thanked the local businesses who'd donated money for the construction materials, Roger hadn't heard that one of them was Beverly Lambert, Realtor, spending money—wastefully, he'd think.

Miranda carried a Tupperware bowl that she immediately put in the refrigerator. "Jell-O salad," she said, unzipping her jacket. "Must have a Jell-O salad. The turkey done?"

"Yes," Mimi said. She pointed to bottles of red wine on the counter. "Chardonnay in the fridge, help yourselves, I'll round up Lloyd," and she ran.

But Bev saw that she didn't turn to go into the living room, she kept on running into the hall. Bev glanced at Roger and Leon heading for the wine, Pauline and Miranda looking in the oven at pans of mashed potatoes, mashed squash, stuffing. Motherly instincts on alert, she went after Mimi, past the workroom inhabited by Mimi's looms and sewing machine, into the showroom, a lovely place of fabrics in many forms. Smooth wooden hangers displayed woven vests, skirts, jackets, ponchos; shelves and open bureau drawers showed handbags, shoulder bags, place mats, scarves, bookmarks. There was a rack of greeting cards that Lloyd made with swatches of Mimi's fabrics; Mimi stood twirling it.

Bev asked, "Darling, what's wrong?"

"Nothing, Mother."

"What's wrong?"

Mimi stopped the rack's spin. "Leicester Printing is going out of business. As of yesterday, after twenty-four years there, Lloyd doesn't have a job."

Bev's stomach went sick. "Oh," she said. "Oh, Mimi."

"You know Lloyd. Mr. Unflappable. I can't decide if he truly thinks he'll find another job or if he's in denial."

"Oh, Mimi, why didn't you phone me, why didn't you cancel this dinner?"

"And disrupt everyone's plans at the last minute and spoil everyone's Thanksgiving? We decided not to mention it until the holiday is over. And hope it's not in the news. Anyway, Etta and Steve and Jeremy were already on the road by the time Lloyd was given the news at five o'clock. I didn't mean to let it slip to you, I didn't mean to bolt, I've got to get back to the kitchen—"

Etta came into the showroom, laughing. "Did I hear our names? Jeremy is up from his nap and watching TV with the guys." Her cascading auburn curls were tousled as if she had also been having a morning nap and had then been too busy with Jeremy to remember to comb it. Or to smooth her T-shirt, on which a palomino galloped through the wrinkles. Bev, because she and this younger daughter looked so much alike, kept seeing herself at previous ages. Now thirty-three, Etta was the editor of the equestrian magazine she'd gone to work for after graduating from Mount Holyoke; at that age, Bev had still been a stay-at-home wife and mother.

Mimi said, "Come, Mother, you say hi to Jeremy and I'll—"

Etta put her hand on Mimi's arm. "Wait. There's news. I don't want to make a dinner announcement à la Daddy—"

Roger was known to pontificate. A baby, Bev thought delightedly, Jeremy is going to have a little sister or brother!

"—so I'll tell you both," Etta said, "and you can tell Daddy and Lloyd later. Thanks to Snowy, I've got an agent!"

"An agent?" Mimi asked.

"Snowy?" Bev asked.

"I swore her to secrecy when I told her I'd written a book, when I asked for her help. She doesn't use an agent, hasn't needed one for her poetry. I've been doing research about agents, I narrowed it down, and I asked her if she'd ask her editor at Wingfield Press about the ones I thought most likely. Wingfield Press doesn't publish murder mysteries, so that wasn't a possibility, I just needed her editor's advice. And Snowy asked her, and the editor narrowed my list down further, and I wrote a query letter, and the first agent I sent it to was interested and has just finished reading it and phoned me yesterday before she left for the holiday, *phoned me*, to say she wants to take it on!"

Glancing at Mimi's flabbergasted expression, Bev thought her own must match.

Etta said, "That's my news."

Bev took a breath. "A murder mystery?"

"It's not Dick Francis," Etta replied, "but it's a murder mystery with horses. A cozy."

Jealousy surged. "Has Snowy read it?"

"She had to, didn't she, so she'd know if it was any good. She couldn't ask her editor to help with something awful." Etta laughed. "Not that Snowy put it that way! I printed a copy for her. She didn't want to read it on her computer. You old folks!"

Bev asked, "May I read it?"

"Snowy's system with poems is not to show them to anybody except Tom until they're in print. But I haven't even shown Steve." A wail from Jeremy. Etta jerked her head toward the door and said, "Gotta go. No announcement, okay? But happy news for you two for Thanksgiving!" She dashed into the hall.

"Dick Francis," Mimi said. "Horse racing."

"Steeple-chasing," Bev said. "The horses in his mysteries mostly do steeple-chasing."

They looked at each other. Then Mimi touched Bev's vest and looked around the room. "Can you tell I haven't had to replenish stock? Nothing is selling."

"Oh, Mimi."

"I must go back to the kitchen. Lloyd isn't keeping his mind on the turkey. Remember how I forgot to cook the turkey for our wedding reception at Snowy's Hurricane Farm? For the buffet I was going to cook the turkey overnight, the way we did back then in the oven, but I forgot, so that morning Snowy and I stuck it in her oven and it cooked while we all climbed Mount Pascataquac for the wedding and when we came down it was done." Mimi's voice wobbled. "A June wedding with hot turkey like Thanksgiving." She ran into the hall.

Bev followed, shocked that Snowy hadn't broken a vow of secrecy to tell her best friend about a cozy mystery written by Snowy's namesake and wondering how could she convince Snowy to lend her the printout to read.

But then there was Jeremy to play with while everybody else worked loading the dining table and Jeremy on his booster seat beside her during the dinner. Not until the younger womenfolk cleared the table for dessert did she have her brainstorm: When she and Snowy had last talked, Snowy had been frantic about the Thetford store, about how she and Ruhamah hadn't yet found a new manager. If Bev could find one, Snowy would owe her!

Standing up, she left Jeremy to Steve, who was discussing the New England Patriots with Leon. In the kitchen, Miranda was holding dessert plates ready as Etta and Pauline sliced pies. Bev went to Mimi at the coffeemaker pouring coffee and said in a low voice, "The manager of the Thetford General Store is getting married and moving to Texas, and Snowy is searching for a replacement. Shall I tell her Lloyd will be looking for a job?"

Mimi stared. She said slowly, "Can you picture Lloyd *managing* anything? But I could manage it."

A phone rang.

"Mine," Pauline said, her voice startled. The phone rang again. She repeated, guardedly this time, "Mine." She delved into her shoulder bag on the kitchen chair and glanced at the phone. Then she dropped the bag on the floor and plopped into the chair. "Hello, Kathy."

Wasn't that her daughter's name?

Roger stepped into the kitchen. Bev looked at him, silently asking if he'd called Pauline's children. He shook his head, mouthed, "Not me," and shrugged.

"Oh," Pauline said to Kathy. "Oh, so your dad finally got around to telling you. Happy Thanksgiving."

# Chapter Three

## 1. Snowy

The time used to be longer between Thanksgiving and Christmas, Snowy thought, driving beside a wide brook the following Wednesday, Mimi in the passenger seat, the morning sunny and cold, Monday's freezing rain having ended in an inch of snow that yesterday had seemed to vanish without melting. Of course the actual number of days between Thanksgiving and Christmas would change depending on how the holidays fell on the calendar, but the feeling of time had always been lengthier, and it wasn't just in childhood. There had been two separate holidays instead of both combined into a Holiday Season.

Now, after Thanksgiving weekend, after taking Mimi to the Thetford store Monday to meet Donna and go over details, and after Mimi's agreeing to replace Donna, she was taking Mimi to the third store, Oakhill, to meet its manager, Cindy O'Donnell, and confer about the stores' plans for Christmas specials. Ye gods, Christmas preparations already, right on the heels of Thanksgiving! Last Friday, Ruhamah had as usual insisted on recognizing this, on immediately undoing the Woodcombe store's Thanksgiving decorations and putting up Christmas. At Thetford, Snowy had seen that Donna had done the same.

Snowy accelerated, starting up a steep hill, and glanced at Mimi looking out the window.

Ruhamah was vastly relieved that Mimi had taken the job. So was Donna—she could quash misgivings, get married, and move to Texas. And fast! Donna and Brian had arranged a small wedding for a week from this Saturday at the Thetford church. But Snowy felt torn; relieved, yes, and happy for Donna and Brian, but she was heartsick that Mimi had to leave Weaverbird, letting Lloyd handle it if any customers should appear.

Mimi said, "I don't think I've ever been over this way before. Is the Oakhill General Store a 'destination' for people?"

"Somewhat, since we bought it." Snowy had earlier explained to Mimi that the Oakhill store's owner, Moose Jackson, like the owners of the Thetford store, had had enough, but unlike the Thetford owners he'd let it run down before he put it up for sale. And then he departed to live with a daughter in Florida.

She reached the hilltop, where a farmhouse and barn stood bare on the horizon, without snow to snuggle into. Not even the smoke from the farmhouse chimney could warm up the scene today. Cows were disconsolately prodding noses at the barnyard's bales of hay. Snowy pictured the Gunthwaite farm where Bev grew up, the white Cape and gray barn, now Harriet's, where at Thanksgiving Harriet had served champagne to celebrate President Obama's election.

Mimi said, "You mentioned that Cindy is like you and Donna, living near the store."

"Yes, on the road that goes past the store." Snowy thought how Mimi would be driving more than an hour from Leicester to Thetford. She added, "Cindy had a lot of enterprises before she took this job. Caning chairs, making jams and jellies, babysitting, and filling in part-time for Moose. Her kids are grown now; one son lives nearby, the other and his wife in Gunthwaite. Wayne, her husband, is the town's road agent."

Down the hill they dropped, past Capes and a Colonial, to the village center. Compared with Thetford's, it always seemed to Snowy like a frontier outpost. An old white clapboard town hall; a newish brick cube of a post office to replace an old one; an A-frame-style church to replace one that had burned; a brick fire station; and Buddy's Auto Service, the grubby garage to which Tom and other devoted guys brought their vehicles. The Oakhill General Store had become equally grubby, a hangout for Moose and his cohorts. But Ruhamah had envisioned its return to being what a general store should be, a gathering place, the heart of the community. And a destination for folks from neighboring towns who needed groceries, coffee, gossip, companionship, as well as for summer people who wanted local color.

Snowy pulled into the small parking lot, where three pick-ups and two SUVs were parked. She unhooked her seat belt. On St. Patrick's Day last March, the store had reopened, revived with white paint and a new and legible sign. She said, "The sign includes a little joke."

OAKHILL GENERAL STORE

YOUR ONE-SHOP STOPPING CENTER

Mimi sat still, looking at the sign, not smiling at the joke. She said, "You had to put aside your work to concentrate on the Woodcombe store when you and Alan bought it. Your poems."

Snowy said gently, "My work wasn't full-time like your weaving and your shop." But she was remembering the abandonment of her writing schedule, the struggle to overcome agoraphobia, leave the house, wait on people. She tried for another joke. "Puddles once told me that although writing poems was my life, it didn't seem to need much time and equipment and expense; I could do it on the backs of old envelopes."

For the first time in these two days they'd spent together, Mimi laughed. "Puddles!"

They got out of the car. Cindy also had switched her decorations over to Christmas, so Santa and his elves were on the big new front window and a wreath adorned the front door. Snowy said, "Cindy makes wreaths, too; she made the one on our Woodcombe store. Let's have the scones she makes from Wayne's grandmother's recipe, they're great."

Mimi asked anxiously, "But Donna doesn't—didn't—bake?"

"No. Don't worry, Mimi, it's not in the job description. Cindy just likes to." Snowy opened the door into the warm smell of coffee, the energetic sound of women's voices. Like the Thetford store, Oakhill was too small for a lunch counter, so the customers were clustered around the little self-service coffee counter, two women and three men all in parkas and jeans, holding Styrofoam cups, with Cindy joining the conversation from behind the meat case where she was arranging logs of bologna, salami, and liverwurst. She wore an Oakhill General Store sweatshirt, of course, a gray one that emphasized the gray in her short dark hair but Cindy wouldn't give a damn about that. She was such a solid and sensible woman that her flirty cat-eye glasses looked startlingly frivolous.

She was saying, "—came back after spending Thanksgiving weekend at her kids' houses, and the trees were gone!"

"I know!" one of the other women said. "How could he *do* that?"

The men shuffled their work boots, and the tallest of them barked a laugh and said, "Well, with a logging crew."

Cindy said, "I heard he hired Jeff—" She spotted Snowy. "Hi, there!" She rushed out from behind the counter. "And you must be Mimi! Everybody, here's the new manager of the Thetford General Store! Mimi and Snowy, come have coffee."

Snowy, imagining she could see Mimi inwardly flinch at this sudden introduction, this announcement of her new career, asked the group, "What's that about a logging crew?"

Cindy hugged Mimi. "Welcome to our general-stores family."

One of the women said to Mimi, "Nice to meet you," and to Snowy, "You know how the Wilsons' house is tucked way back in the woods?"

The other woman said, "It isn't anymore!"

Cindy herded Mimi and Snowy to the coffee counter, asking Snowy, "You know they were in the midst of a divorce?"

Trying to remember the Wilsons' house, Snowy stalled, saying, "Your scones, I've sung their praises to Mimi."

The first woman said, "Vicki is getting the house in the divorce—"

The second woman finished, "—and while she was away last weekend Barry had the woods cut down."

The men shuffled their work boots again. One said rather admiringly, "Logged right off," and another said, "Stripped, the house open to the road." Then all three said, "Gotta go," tossed their cups into the waiting wastebasket, and left.

The first woman sighed, "I should be on my way too," and hoisted a tote bag she must've brought, environmentally conscious. Then she glanced from the tote bag to Mimi and exclaimed, "You're Weaverbird!"

Mimi was accepting a cup of coffee and a paper plate with a scone on it from Cindy. She looked up, startled.

The woman said, "I bought a tote bag at your shop! Not this everyday one, but a lovely one. Will you still be weaving if you're running the Thetford store?"

Mimi held the cup and paper plate. "Yes."

The second woman said to Cindy, "I guess it'll be a pound of hamburg. Anything except turkey."

"Too true." Cindy handed Snowy a cup of coffee and a plate of scone, returned to the meat counter, and resumed speculation about the Wilsons. "Will Vicki sue him, is that possible?"

The first woman said, "Whatever, it won't resurrect those woods."

Snowy said to Mimi, "Speaking of logging, come see the porch," and led her down an aisle toward the back door. On their way here she'd told Mimi how, when Bev was showing her this store for sale, Cindy had come in to find out what was going on and had dragged them down to the back of the store to describe her idea for a back porch. Right at that moment a logging truck had crashed into the front of the store. If they'd still been standing there . . . Ruhamah, to thank Cindy for saving Snowy's and Bev's lives, had had the porch built and named it Cindy's Porch.

At the back door, Snowy stopped. Too cold to sit on the porch today, and anyway, the tables and chairs had been brought in for the winter. So she and Mimi gazed out the door's window, at the empty porch and the golden-brown brook curving across the brown field.

Snowy said, "You can change your mind about Thetford, Mimi. You could hunt for something else, something closer to Leicester."

"Working at a mall store?"

"Can you think of Thetford as temporary, until Lloyd finds a job?"

Mimi set her cup down on a nearby shelf. "No," she said, and took a bite of her scone.

## 2. Snowy

Snowy remembered Bev's telling her how she'd sat in the backseat of her Subaru with a pie basket when she and Roger and Pauline went to Mimi and Lloyd's for Thanksgiving. Now on this Thursday, en route to Ruhamah and D. J.'s this sunny Christmas morning, Snowy sat in the passenger seat of her Subaru holding a cake-carrier containing the applesauce cake she'd made last evening from the recipe given to her by Alan's mother, who had always made an applesauce cake at Christmas instead of a fruitcake. Tom drove, wearing his woolen Forbes-tartan tam at a jaunty angle. As with the timing of Bev's Thanksgiving at Mimi's, their Christmas visit was timed between naps. Al's naps, in this instance. They would have dinner first, Ruhamah had decreed, and open presents second, which Al could sleep through if he decided to.

It was a white Christmas, Sunday's latest big snowstorm having brought another foot of snow—or two, depending on drifting. Today's windy weather was whipping up white spirals on the fields they passed and on Woodcombe Lake. Tom turned off onto Thorne Road, a jouncy dirt road known locally as the Roller Coaster Road. When they neared Hurricane Farm she tried to see only Rita's Christmas wreath and not think of the Christmases she and Alan and Ruhamah had celebrated in that old white farmhouse. The big wreath on the front door sported red and green bows, silver bells, and many-colored shiny plastic fruit.

Snowy observed, "Rita is going all out as usual." But since her husband's death, Rita and her granddaughter, Mallory, spent Christmas Day at Rita's sister's down in Somersworth.

Tom observed, "She should get her roof cleared off."

On Tuesday David had tended to the North Country Coffins roof with roof rake and snow shovel. He had taken over this chore from Tom even before Tom's knee replacements last February, but Snowy knew Tom still was feeling that he himself ought to be able to do it instead of his son. A big jounce jolted the cake-carrier up from her lap. She settled it and said, "Al's great-grandmother's presence. Jumping for joy that I've made her applesauce cake. And that Ruhamah's baby is a boy."

She had succeeded in distracting Tom from his brooding. He shot her a glance and grinned. "And Al will jump for joy that you're giving him a book."

"He certainly will." The book was *Charlotte's Web*, now that she'd finished reading him *Stuart Little* while babysitting. She'd also sung him Pete Seeger's version of E. B. White's poem "The Spider's Web." But at the end of everything, she always concluded with the lullaby her mother had sung her:

> Sail away to Blanket Bay
> And return at break of day . . .

How those two words, "Blanket Bay," had appealed to her in her own childhood, when they grew from mere sounds to words, an image! As Al fell asleep, she'd whisper to him, "Can you say 'alliteration'?"

Books. Etta's murder mystery. The working title Etta had chosen was from a Robert Browning poem: *Boot, Saddle, to Horse, and Away*. Bev's hints were getting broader about borrowing Snowy's printout. Snowy kept saying she'd misplaced it. She hated lying to Bev, but she certainly understood Etta's desire for privacy. As she herself had realized early on, if you worried about whether or not your parents and friends would approve of what you wrote (especially sex), you'd never write a word. She'd sensed that Bev thought Snowy should feel obliged to comply because Bev had rescued her by suggesting Mimi for the Thetford store. Gripping the cake-carrier, Snowy tried to toughen her heart and conscience, for the sake of art.

The road continued through the woods, the route she used to jog each morning from Hurricane Farm to the Thorne farm, now Ruhamah and D. J.'s.

Tom mused, “Too bad the hardware store doesn’t still have toys.”

“Yes.” In their youth, at Christmastime at the Gunthwaite Hardware Store on Main Street, space had been cleared on the second floor for Santa’s Workshop, a big display of toys, naturally enough featuring those for boys but also including dolls, doll houses—and a little-girl-size kitchen she still remembered yearning over. She said to Tom what she always said when he and she got to reminiscing about Santa’s Workshop, “I’m positive we must’ve been there together when our folks brought us, only we didn’t know. We had to wait until high school to meet.”

“What a waste,” he said, as he always did.

They laughed.

He pulled into Ruhamah and D. J.’s driveway, a plowed slot between snowbanks. Invisible in the barn were Ruhamah’s Toyota pickup and D. J.’s some-kind-of-SUV. Ruhamah and D. J., Snowy thought, really did save the old weather-beaten farmhouse and barn, rejuvenated with paint outside and cleaned up within. The white Cape and red barn both had Cindy-made wreaths on their doors; this year Ruhamah had also attached a Cindy wreath to her pickup’s hood, a rare flight of silliness (Al’s influence?). Remembering the work that Mimi and Lloyd had put into saving their old farmhouse, Snowy pictured Lloyd spending his days now puttering aimlessly there while Mimi worked at the Thetford store. D. J.’s job couldn’t be called secure, but it would be for two more years. Knock on wood.

Tom opened his door, pushing hard against the wind. “Jesus. Let me get your door.” He clambered out, then clamped down his tam. "Shit!" Like a mime walking slantwise against an imaginary gale, he walked around the front of the car to her door, wrenched it open, and helped her out, appropriating the cake-carrier. From inside the house, Kaylie the border collie was giving alert barks to announce their arrival.

Snowy yanked the cake-carrier back and gasped into the wind, "Thanks, but you'll have your hands full with the presents."

Tom opened the backseat door and lifted out the Mimi-made tote bags of Christmas-wrapped presents, including those sent for Al from Santa's elves in Florida, Alan's sister and brother-in-law. He and Snowy battled their way up the shoveled path to the back of the house, stomped their boots on the doorstep, and crossed the porch, where firewood was stacked.

D. J. opened the back door into the low-ceilinged kitchen and the aroma of turkey pie. "Welcome!"

He looked like Dudley, tall, blond, rosy. Kaylie nudged him aside for greetings, and amid this confusion he took the tote bags from Tom, hugged Snowy and took the cake-carrier, and began to sing, warbling, "*Mon beau sapin*—" He paused.

The French version of "O Tannenbaum"! Patting Kaylie, Snowy laughed. "Your father's favorite carol. We learned it in French class."

D. J.'s face clouded. "Yes. Yes, it is."

Puzzled, Snowy said, "Continue. I promise I won't join in."

D. J. hesitated, then sang, "*Que j'aime ta verdure*—"

But from the living room Ruhamah interrupted, calling, "Come see the *sapin*!"

The Christmas tree, Al's first Christmas tree. Snowy hung her parka on a kitchen peg and quickly smoothed down the very first Christmas sweater she'd ever owned, bought this winter in honor of Al, a red one with green letters across the front that said Mrs. Claus. She sat down in the rocker, unlaced her boots, pulled them off, straightened her red wool socks, and placed the boots beside Cleora Thorne's wood cookstove even though it wasn't in use anymore and couldn't dry them. Ruhamah had turned it into a houseplant stand; its array included a Christmas cactus that this year had bloomed on Columbus Day. The gas range's oven window showed the Indulgences turkey pie being heated up. She hurried with the tote bags into the living room. In these low rooms the winter sunlight was compressed, intensified, but it didn't dim the red and green lights on the Christmas tree or the fire flickering in the little brick fireplace. The tree and fire scents were vying for predominance, fresh balsam and burning beech. Of the Thornes' living-room furniture that the Thorne kids hadn't wanted, Ruhamah had kept the 1950s blond coffee table.

Of Snowy's furnishings, Ruhamah had hoseyed the Oriental rug and Alan's wing chair. The sofa they'd bought. Ruhamah sat on it, holding Al cuddled in her left arm and a booklet in her right hand. Al was looking at the tree, trimmed with most of Snowy's accumulation of decorations, now new for him. Could Al be focused on the red china cardinal? He was wearing a red sweater over a green onesie, and his booties were reindeer, the outfit an early Christmas present that Snowy hadn't been able to resist.

"Merry Christmas," Snowy said, stooping to kiss Al. She kissed Ruhamah and saw that the booklet was from the town's historical society. "Is Al getting interested in Woodcombe's history?"

"I was checking something. It's the issue about the buildings on Main Street."

"Oh, yes, your father and I read it decades ago." Snowy knelt with the tote bags and added the presents to those already under the tree. She had done most of her Christmas shopping at Weaverbird: a poncho for Ruhamah, yet another tie for D. J., and yet another blanket for Al in addition to *Charlotte's Web*. Then she struggled to rise without grabbing at the tree for support.

Ruhamah dropped the booklet, jumped up, and held out her empty hand. "I was thinking about what to do at our stores to welcome the New Year—"

Loathing the necessity, Snowy clutched her hand and stood.

"—and all of a sudden I realized that next year might be the Woodcombe store's one-hundred-and-fiftieth anniversary, so I checked and it is. The store opened on March fourteenth, eighteen fifty-nine. We should do something special. A sesquicentennial party, of course, but also something permanent."

Snowy remembered reading about how Joshua Bickford had opened the store in March 1859. She and Alan had imagined the customers, farmers and farm wives looking forward to the spring but exhausted by winter and wondering if they had the energy for another spring planting. Had Joshua Bickford been terrified of failure, as she and Alan had been?

Ruhamah was saying, "How about making a time capsule?"

From the kitchen came the buzz of a stove timer. D. J. called, "It's done!"

Ruhamah smiled. "My simplest Christmas menu ever. The Indulgences pie, the store's coleslaw—and you brought Phyllis's cake?" She jiggled Al and told him, "Your great-grandmother always made a special cake and now your grandmother does."

"Eek, scones, I forgot to tell you I brought scones too!" Snowy bent—didn't kneel again—and snatched up one of the Christmas packages, gilt with a green bow. "Don't let Kaylie devour this. You weren't at the store when Cindy brought her scones yesterday, a bag for you and D. J. and one for Tom and me. Your Boxing Day breakfast tomorrow. Keeping things simple."

Ruhamah took the bag and looked at it, looked at her. "Cindy's grandmother-in-law's recipe. That's it! Recipes! That's how we'll celebrate the store's sesquicentennial, we'll do a cookbook!"

"A cookbook?"

"You know, one of those self-published community collections of recipes, and we can include the Thetford and Oakhill stores and sell copies there too!"

Snowy asked Al, "Isn't your mother brilliant?" and transferred him into her own arms, cradling him close.

## 3. Bev

THE WIND OFF THE LAKE WAS LOUD, WATERLIGHT WAS CREAKING mightily, and the furnace was whooshing heat to add to the warmth from the living room's big fireplace, above which Teddy looked content with the winter sunlight and with children and grown-ups clamoring and a canary singing as Roger distributed presents from under the Christmas tree. But through all this racket Bev heard the doorbell. She glanced at her watch—almost one o'clock—and then at Pauline in a wicker chair exclaiming over an unopened Yvonne's Apparel box (containing a present from Roger, a canary-yellow sweater Bev had chosen). Dandy, beside her in his cage hanging from the stand that Roger had bought him when Pauline moved in, certainly seemed to be enjoying the festivities too. No, Pauline hadn't heard the doorbell. The person ringing it must be Kathy, Pauline's daughter, due here just about now.

Well, she herself was the hostess. Bev stood and slipped out of the room, knowing that today she still looked less than decorative even though she was wearing her lovely silvery sweater and derriere-flattering black pants. Nerved-up was how she'd looked in the bedroom full-length mirror when she'd changed into hostess clothes after working in the kitchen with Pauline.

The aroma of Christmas dinner permeated the house, the turkey cooking by the good old-fashioned method of the kitchen stove's oven and timed for 2 p.m. after the opening of presents. She hurried to the hallway. As usual she had decorated it with poinsettias, mistletoe, garlands of evergreens, and from the ceiling hung Puddles's present: kissing balls! Two of them, of course. For some unknown reason, Christmas seasons lately had brought a new item to greenhouses and supermarkets in addition to Christmas wreaths, these so-called kissing balls. What was wrong with simple mistletoe? Snowy had Googled and then reported that they were an updated version of a traditional ball of herbs and evergreens. The name of course had delighted Puddles, who now sent a pair each Christmas to dear friends Snowy and Bev. As Snowy remarked, kissing balls seemed to have replaced malt balls in Puddles's heart. Bev opened the front door.

The wind pushed a young woman headlong into the hallway. Young, that is, in comparison. Her suitcase swung forward and bumped Bev.

Bev took the suitcase. "Kathy?" She hadn't seen Pauline's children since they still were children and living at home. Kathy was the oldest; age forty-seven Pauline had told her after Kathy's Thanksgiving phone call. Bev had unabashedly listened to Pauline's side of that brief conversation, but it was mostly monosyllabic—"Yes." "No."— until the end, when Pauline had glanced at Bev and then said, "Remember to wear and pack warm clothes." Afterward, Pauline had explained that Kathy had invited herself to Waterlight for Christmas, would fly from Atlanta to Boston, spend the night in a hotel, and drive to Gunthwaite Christmas morning.

"Yup," the young woman said, "I'm Kathy."

"Welcome," Bev said. "Merry Christmas. I'm Bev."

Kathy said, "I remember who you are, Aunt Bev."

Aunt? Oh, good Lord, yes, aunt-by-marriage. She had forgotten that Roger's nieces and nephews called her "aunt." Disconcertingly, Kathy looked a little like Leon; no, like both Roger and Leon. Similar eyebrows. Kathy had Pauline's original dark hair, hers in a wind-disheveled bun. She was wearing a light wool coat and perky low boots, not much protection in this weather, so she hadn't heeded Pauline's warning. Driving from Boston, she wouldn't have been exposed much to the elements, but what if she'd had a car accident or otherwise found herself stranded outdoors? Her slender shoulder bag at least must contain a cell phone. Bev decided that an aunt-in-law should hug a niece-in-law, so she set down the suitcase and did so, asking, "How was your trip?"

Kathy smiled a nice white smile, reminding Bev that Pauline had mentioned that Kathy was the receptionist in a dentists' big office, had been for years, and, according to Pauline, ran the place, bossing around hygienists *and* dentists. Pauline had also volunteered the reminder that Kathy was divorced, a single mother of a daughter and son in their twenties, the daughter married. Kathy said, "My kids think I'm crazy to travel on a holiday to check on their grandmother."

Their grandmother, Bev thought, had needed checking on since Halloween. She said, "Let me hang up your coat. We'll leave your suitcase here. Your bedroom is upstairs, the room we call Wood Duck. For now, let's join the family in the living room."

Kathy unbuttoned her coat, revealing a practical dark blue dress. "What has Mom told you?"

"Told me?"

"Told you and Uncle Roger about what happened."

Bev stared at her. "Um, this is something to discuss with them, isn't it? Your mother and Roger."

Kathy handed her the coat, unzipped the suitcase, removed a small book-shaped Christmas-wrapped package, zipped it shut. She inhaled. "Dinner smells good." She pointed at the stack of firewood beside the front door. "And I smell wood smoke too."

"Yes." Bev carried the coat over to the hall closet and repeated, "Let's join the family."

"There are two sides to every story," Kathy began, then fell silent. She followed Bev into the living room, where she blurted, "What on earth is that, a moose?"

"His name is Teddy." Bev surveyed the scene: the vast room beneath the evergreens-decorated balcony; the appetizers buffet on the wicker tea cart she'd found in an antiques store; the big tree dotted with the tiny white lights she'd bought a couple of years ago when there was money for new decorating experiments (Money! Eight years ago at Christmas she had given Roger a five-hundred-dollar briefcase, showing off her real-estate affluence); and the family assembled together—Dick and Jessica and, looking adorable in turtlenecks, skirts, and tights in combinations of red and green, little Abigail and Felicity; Mimi and Lloyd; Leon and Miranda; Pauline and Dandy. No Etta, Steve, and Jeremy, who were at Steve's parents' in Massachusetts. No Trulianne and Clem, who were at Trulianne's parents' in Eastbourne. Keeping her eyes on Pauline, she projected her voice to a theater range: "Kathy is here!"

Pauline had finally asked Bev for the name of her salon, and her hair was back to pixie-cut brunette, but despite this preparation for the meeting she didn't leap up and rush to hug her daughter.

Kathy crossed to her, bent down, and hugged her. Then held out the package. "Merry Christmas, Mom. Hi there, Dandy."

The tiny white lights on the Christmas tree went out. The furnace fell silent.

Panic gripped Bev. The electricity had gone off! Then she remembered that this summer they had finally made the horribly expensive purchase of a generator, which Roger had called a necessity for a B-and-B. And when the next thunderstorm had caused the electricity to go off, he had been very proud that the generator immediately, as he put it, kicked in.

She looked at Roger. He was waiting.

Dick stood up. Years ago his once-red hair had gone prematurely gray, as hers had before continuing on to prematurely white. "Dad, I thought you mentioned that you'd bought a generator?"

Roger said, "It was working Monday. It does a self-check for twenty minutes every Monday afternoon. I'll phone Stan."

Involuntarily, Bev objected, "On Christmas, Roger?" Stan, their amiable electrician, had installed the generator.

Roger asked her, "Do you want the fucking house to freeze up?" and pulled his cell phone out of a pocket of his corduroys and strode out of the room.

Jessica didn't have a chance to cover Abigail's and Felicity's ears against the f-word. In fact, she didn't seem to have noticed. Jessica might appear to be a languid blonde, but she had worked at a Manhattan public-relations firm until the arrival of Abigail and she was briskly competent, down-to-earth. She asked Dick, "Should we all start bringing in more firewood?" And counting to herself she said, "There's this fireplace, and the one in the suite and the one in Bev and Roger's bedroom."

Bev stood rooted. The suite! Their two lone B-and-B guests were staying in the suite! The son and daughter-in-law of Russell, the Gunthwaite Summer Theater's director, they were having

Christmas with Russell and his wife and the rest of that family but they'd be back here tonight! Toilets, she thought. No water without electricity so you can't flush toilets. She used to keep jugs of water stored for these emergencies, but with the advent of the generator she hadn't bothered. They could melt snow in pails in front of the fireplaces—

Felicity, age three, said, "I'm hungry. For dinner."

The turkey! The stove was a gas stove, but Bev started running, down the corridor past the dining room where she had set the table this morning with place mats woven at different times by Mother and Mimi, into the kitchen. Years ago she had painted it in pale greens and blues, soothing colors that should calm her down now, but her heart kept pounding, and as she looked wildly around at all the dinner preparations to be completed she felt as if she might disintegrate. Too much, too much! The stove would finish cooking the turkey, but there would be no water, hot or cold, for all the other work. She had to boil and mash the potatoes, make the gravy—

Arriving in the kitchen behind her, Felicity persisted, "I'm hungry, Gaga."

This was the nickname that Clem had given her, which the other grandchildren had adopted. Now exhaustion engulfed Bev.

Felicity became precise. "I want dinner. Not more nibblies."

Jessica appeared. "Sweetie, the turkey isn't quite ready yet. The stove's timer has to buzz." She opened the fridge and took out a jar. "We'll have peanut butter and jelly."

Felicity roared, "*I want Christmas dinner!*"

The wind shook the house.

Kathy marched into the kitchen, opened the oven, studied the turkey and the pan of extra stuffing beside it. Then unerringly she opened the correct cupboard, the correct drawer, and took out a plate, a spoon, a fork. She was, Bev realized, one of those lucky women who were at once at home in other people's kitchens. Kathy plopped a scoop of stuffing onto the plate. "There," she said, putting the plate and fork on the table. "We all really just want stuffing, don't we."

Laughing, Jessica yanked a pillow off the bentwood rocker, set it on a pastel green chair at the pastel blue kitchen table, and hoisted Felicity onto it. "Thank you, Kathy. Bev, could you keep an eye on her? The others are going to lug more firewood from the woodshed to the hallway, and I'll help."

As Jessica left the kitchen, Pauline hurried in. "Look," she said grimly, thrusting something at Bev while glaring at Kathy, "look what Kathy brought me for Christmas."

Unwrapped, the present was a charred bundle smelling like smoke—and not the comfy smell of wood smoke. Bev touched it. The remains of a book with a padded cover. When she carefully lifted the cover she saw the blackened remains of a photograph. The book was a photograph album. A wedding album, the first photo showing a bride and groom who must be Pauline and Greg. Bev remembered attending the wedding in Gunthwaite's St. Mary's church. She asked Kathy, "You found it after the fire?"

Kathy settled in at the table beside Felicity. "Dad did. He piled up what he salvaged, for me to go through." To Felicity she said, "I'm Kathy, your grandfather's niece, which makes us, let's see, well, let's say we're cousins. What's your name?"

Felicity swallowed stuffing. "Felicity Beverly Lambert."

Bev asked, "So you've been to Wartling to visit your father? You and your brothers?"

"Just me," Kathy said. "They're too busy and far away, so they say. As if I'm not busy, and I don't live all that close."

Pauline opened the oven and peered in. "Of course *he* didn't want the album."

"Mom," Kathy said, "he's a man. They deal with things differently."

Pauline opened a cupboard. "Paper plates. We can say the hell with dinner and just make sandwiches."

Bev exploded, "For God's sake, what is Greg doing? Where is he living? What about the insurance? Is he going to rebuild the family home or buy another house or what? When can Pauline return to some sort of home? This has gone on long enough!"

Felicity looked up from her empty plate. Damn, Bev thought, have I frightened her?

Kathy said, "He's rented a condo. He likes it. The simple life."

Pauline asked, "What makes you think I want to return?"

Bev held out the album, her hands shaking. "This! Your wedding!"

"So?" Pauline said. "If I'm remembering right, you took a long vacation from your husband."

And into the kitchen—as if on cue!—Roger sauntered, looking pleased with himself. "Stan will be right over to get the generator going."

Bev cried, "But Stan's Christmas will be spoiled!"

"Oh, I don't know," Roger said. "He's coming to the rescue. Some guys like to do that. And he said he was ready for a break from too much family."

Felicity patted her stomach. "Room for dessert."

The stove's timer began buzzing.

## 4. Bev

"OKAY," PAULINE SAID, HAULING OUT THE ROASTING PAN, "STAN OR NO Stan, the meal is still going to be casual. Sandwiches. Don't bother waiting for the turkey to set, Roger, just carve. We'll skip the potatoes, potato chips instead, skip the gravy, make it later, these will be plain sandwiches, not hot open-face and needing silverware—"

This is *my* kitchen, Bev thought, I'm the one in charge—

Roger grabbed his parka off a peg. "I'd better go wait for Stan." He opened the back door onto the porch, and the wind barged in. He disappeared around the corner of the house.

"Men," Pauline said.

Felicity said, "Dessert!"

Kathy stood up, saying to Felicity, "First I'm going to carve the turkey and then we'll have a picnic." She unhesitatingly opened the knife drawer.

"Kathy," Bev said, "you told me there are two sides to every story."

Pauline said, "Ha!"

"Picnic," Felicity said, starting to struggle down from her chair.

Bev tossed the album on the table, lifted her granddaughter up before she fell, and collapsed in the chair, hugging Felicity's solid warmth.

"Gaga," said Felicity, cuddling.

Warmth, Bev thought. Were Snowy and her family warm and okay or had the electricity gone off in Woodcombe too? Snowy and Ruhamah didn't have generators in their homes, but the store did and they could take refuge there. Bev remembered doing so herself, during the Ice Storm of 1998. However, she should phone Snowy at Ruhamah's and find out and if necessary offer Waterlight, if Stan got the generator going.

She realized that Felicity had dozed off and that Kathy, carving, was saying to Pauline, "Dad says that you didn't take responsibility for not cleaning the lint trap."

Pauline slammed a paper plate onto the counter as if she wished it were china and would break. "Who *always* cleans the lint trap, who taught you to clean the lint trap every time you use the dryer? Me! I *did* clean the lint trap! Whose responsibility was it to clean the hose periodically? His!"

Kathy stopped carving and slowly set aside the knife. "He thinks he's a joke in town now. People are making fun of him, finding it funny. Not funny funny but mean funny. An electrician whose house burns down. It's almost like a fireman whose house burns down. Or a cop whose police car gets stolen by the person he's arresting."

"Kathy," Pauline said, "he abandoned me in the dark in a motel room. He turned off the lights as he went out. I was blind as a bat. I tripped, I could've broken my neck trying to find the light switch."

"He what?" Kathy said.

"It was our second night in the motel. The first night, after all that, the fire and everything, we were in shock. The next day they tell us it started in the laundry room, the dryer. And that night Greg tells me to go live with my brother."

"Oh, Mom. But didn't you think to help him save face? You could've said you couldn't remember when you last cleaned the lint trap."

Pauline slammed down another paper plate. "I admitted I was wrong, I told him and the firemen the dryer was going when I went off to do errands and have lunch."

"Yes, Dad told me you'd left the dryer on. Why? You taught me never to do that."

"I was in a hurry. I confessed, I told the truth, and I told the truth about the lint trap!"

Bev carried sleeping Felicity out of the kitchen, along the corridor. She heard the stomping of boots and thunk of wood in the hallway and then saw Jessica and Dick and even Abigail, as well as Mimi and Lloyd and Miranda and Leon, all depositing armloads of wood. She waved at Jessica, pointed to Felicity and mouthed, "Nap," and went up the staircase.

Jessica and Dick had the Heron Room; Abigail and Felicity had Etta's old room, now Merganser, sharing the queen-size double bed. She eased open the Velcro on Felicity's suede Mary Janes and slid them off—so cute!—and tucked her in. She stood, listening to the house contracting with cold. And then she hurried down the hall to the unnamed bedroom still hers and Roger's and crossed through the jumble of furniture to her cell phone in its charger on her bureau. No electricity, but it should still be charged. She tapped in Snowy's number and waited for Snowy to find her shoulder bag and phone—oh, hell, she'd managed not to awaken Felicity during the trip upstairs but would she now be awakening Al?

Snowy said, "Bev?"

"Did I wake Al?"

"I don't think so. He and Ruhamah are upstairs napping, and Tom and I are about to head home."

"Do you have electricity? Ours has gone off."

"We do here, but I don't know about our place. This wind! I envy you that generator."

"Well, it isn't working, but Stan the generator man is coming to the rescue. Sometimes I think Mother had the right idea, moving to Florida. Despite hurricanes." The health of Fred, Bev's stepfather, had been the reason behind the decision to move. Bev sat down suddenly on the bed. "Snowy, I know it's trite, but I miss Mother even more during holidays."

"It's not trite, Bev."

And Bev knew Snowy had loved Mother too. "I keep worrying about how sad Mother would feel about Mimi's having to give up weaving." Bev added hastily, "But Mother would be grateful that you needed a manager at the Thetford store and so am I." She changed the subject. "How did Al like *Charlotte's Web*?"

"Oh, he was riveted as I read."

"The electricity went off before we finished opening our presents. Everything's all mixed up."

"Did Pauline's daughter arrive?"

Mothers and daughters. "They're now talking—sort of—in the kitchen. I retreated."

"How are your B-and-B guests?"

"In a way I'm relieved we have only two to deal with. Roger is disappointed. But he's elated that we've got three couples coming for New Year's, and I certainly welcome the money, but it'll be a lot of work—and what if the power goes off again and the generator breaks down again?"

"Dick Francis said that 'What if' is the beginning of fiction."

Dick Francis, Bev thought. And in the following silence she suspected that Snowy was thinking: Oh shit, I've mentioned a horsey mystery. Bev didn't ignore this opening; she asked, "Have you found your printout of Etta's book yet?"

"Not yet," Snowy said. "My office is such a mess lately."

Bev had seen Snowy's office many times and it was usually neat as a pin. She decided to mention Mother again, to invoke Mother. "I'm just curious about whether or not Etta has a mother in her book, and I'm sure Mother would be curious too. If there's a heroine and the heroine has a mother."

Snowy said, "Speaking of books, Ruhamah had a brainstorm. The store's one-hundred-and-fiftieth birthday is coming up in March, and besides a party she wants to celebrate it with a cookbook. You know, one of those community-type cookbooks. Would you like to contribute the recipe for your famous meat loaf?"

Snowy was trying to distract her. Bev gave up and replied, "Can I? I don't live in your community."

"The book will include Thetford and Oakhill, and you're related to the Thetford store's manager, so I proclaim that you can be a guest contributor. I guess Puddles can't be, and won't this annoy her!"

"Have you heard from Puddles? Aren't she and Blivit down in South Carolina for Christmas?" To have a base near her children and grandchildren, Puddles had kept the Hilton Head house in which she and Guy, her first husband, had lived.

Snowy called, "Okay, Tom, just a sec," and to Bev she said, "Gotta go. I haven't heard from her since before she left, when she sent our kissing balls and called me to say they were en route and wouldn't you and I be thrilled again this year."

"Ye gods, Puddles!" Bev said.

So they were laughing when they said good-bye.

# Chapter Four

# 1. Snowy

*Banditry.* A flock of chickadees was called a *banditry*, because of chickadees' black masks. Standing at the kitchen stove, Snowy looked out the window at the chickadees zooming from a white pine to the sunflower-seed tube hanging on the bird-feeder pole in the backyard. Earlier on this cold New Year's Day morning (one degree below zero), she had run outdoors and filled the feeder. Now the little bandits were busily lowering the level of the seeds, flying back and forth between the feeder and the pine, where they alighted, switched the seeds from tiny beaks to tiny claws, and with those beaks banged and banged each open. Surely the calories in a sunflower seed couldn't replace the energy spent to crack it?

Down there in the yard, under the snow the hay-mulched garden awaited spring. Soon seed catalogs would arrive in the mail, usually a happy harbinger. But last summer her scoliosis had made gardening more pain than pleasure. Well, she would tough it out.

She returned her attention to the stove. Stew always tasted better the second day, but she hadn't made it yesterday because the store was open on New Year's Eve day and by evening she was too tired to assemble anything lengthy. For supper last night they had celebrated New Year's Eve and Scotland's Hogmanay with an easy little tradition she'd invented after their trip to Scotland: sandwiches of smoked salmon on buttered rye bread. And later in the evening, while they watched a couple of episodes of the library's *As Time Goes By* DVD collection, there was a dram of Tom's Scotch, though they didn't stay up to toast the new year. When had they last done that? Decades ago! The store was closed on New Year's Day. Thus, while Tom in his wing chair was reading *AARP The Magazine* and sipping coffee from his sleeping-with-a-grandmother mug, she was making the other part of her invented tradition, New Year's Day lamb stew, dredging cubes of lamb in flour and browning them in her biggest skillet, prodding the cubes with her tongs, readying the stew in the morning to sit in the fridge until supper.

Suddenly Tom asked, "What was that line of Lionel's last night about aging?"

Snowy reflected. During *As Time Goes By*, Tom had laughed out loud at one of the hero's observations. She replied, "Lionel said something about how he's becoming quite content with doing nothing very slowly."

Tom didn't laugh this morning. He sipped his coffee. Then he remarked, his tone sounding oddly wistful, "If I'd stuck with teaching, I'd be doing that now. Retired. Not still lugging lumber at my age."

Snowy spun around from the stove. "You've reassured me that David is doing the lugging."

"Yes, mostly. But you know what I mean."

She turned back to the stove, not sure that she did. Even after all these years, he could still startle her. Wistful? For what, for more than a retirement income? Did he miss teaching? Did he miss his home in Newburgh with Joanne? Did he miss Joanne—and her teacher's retirement income? Joanne had remarried, and Victor, her husband and Gunthwaite High School classmate, had also retired—he'd worked for some computer company downstate in Nashua—so, combined, they must be comfortable. They had those incomes, their Nashua house, and for getaways to the mountains they had the Newburgh house—

"However," Tom said, "if I'd stuck with teaching I'd've dropped dead of a heart attack caused by dealing with the school administration."

That sounded more like Tom. But she poked at the cubes, worrying. She'd have to ask David if he thought Tom was doing too much. And what about Tom's work at the Mount Pascataquac fire tower? He couldn't work there last year after his knee replacements, but he planned to be hiking up to the tower this spring for his stints as a lookout. The job had no age limit. Years ago he'd told her a tale he'd been told about how back in the 1930s a fire warden on one of New Hampshire's mountains had died in the cab, the little room atop fire towers; getting the unfortunate man down the tower and mountain had been quite a chore, but it was made a little easier because the Civilian Conservation Corps had just completed a road to the summit. Hooray for FDR and the CCC!

Last April, at the end of their two weeks on Quarry Island, she had daydreamed about retiring to Quarry Island in general and Cotter Cottage in particular. Walking along the shore one afternoon while Tom was volunteering at the island's one-room schoolhouse, she had daydreamed and fantasized until she jolted herself back to reality: Her grandson lived in Woodcombe, and anyway, thanks to their financial situation she and Tom couldn't buy the cottage, couldn't retire. But now the daydream resurfaced. Maybe Tom could substitute at the island school and get paid for it, maybe he could build things for people (not just coffins), maybe she could—what could she do? Manage the island store?

Al was in Woodcombe.

She decided that the cubes had browned enough, transferred them to the Dutch oven, added fat-free broth, brought it to a boil, turned it down to a simmer, and set the stove timer for forty-five minutes.

On New Year's Day 2002, Puddles had married Blivit on Quarry Island, in the little granite church whose steeple was topped with a weathervane shaped like a fish. So today was their seventh anniversary. They always flew home from Hilton Head to celebrate their anniversary in Maine. And to get ready to go back to work; Blivit had retired from the CEO position at his family's ice-cream company but had stayed with the Research and Development he loved. Snowy stepped over to the coffeemaker, refilled her rooster mug, and said, "I'm going to phone Puddles and wish her and Blivit a happy anniversary."

Tom looked up from his magazine. "God, that day was cold. Their wedding day."

Unlike their own hot and humid June wedding day. Snowy said, "I guess being surrounded by ocean made it seem extra cold." She laughed. "And then they went off to *Canada* for their honeymoon!"

"Grand Manan Island," Tom recalled. "Islands."

"Puddles will ask me again when we're coming for our honeymoon. Remember, in her Christmastime phone call she told me Mildred Cotter is still in the nursing home and the cottage is still empty."

At the time, Tom hadn't said anything. Today he said, "We're into winter. Mildred will have had it closed up for winter."

"Can't it be opened? It's winterized."

"Sure, but there's only that propane heater and the fireplace in the living room and the electric heater in the bathroom."

Snowy remembered how cold he had been there at first.

He and his accountant handled the finances of his coffin business. She handled their personal finances, and nowadays Ruhamah and their accountant mostly handled the general stores' finances. Mildred Cotter had charged $500 a week for her cottage. Off-season rates, presumably.

She said, "It's our *honeymoon.* We resolved that one way or another, in Cotter Cottage or some other cottage, we would honeymoon on Quarry Island."

"Maybe it would make more sense to wait until spring."

She recalled that Blivit's Aunt Izzy, who lived year-round in the family's castle on the island, had remarked last April,

"Although on the island it seems we keep even busier in the winter than in the summer, visiting and suppers and playing cards and sewing and knitting, volleyball in the town hall and skating on the pond, and it's the time to repair traps . . . yet winter can still begin to gnaw at you." It could gnaw at you inland too, but it wasn't so isolated, claustrophobic, unless you were snowed in.

Tom looked up at her, blue eyes anxious, eyes far bluer than her own.

Was he changing his mind about the honeymoon simply because he was worried about the cold and the cost? She thought of the hassle of packing, of driving to Long Harbor, spending the night at Puddles and Blivit's house, having them take her and Tom to the dock, lugging luggage to the ferry, the boat trip, unloading onto the Quarry Island dock, transferring everything to Blivit's island Jeep Wagoneer that Blivit would loan them, driving to Cotter Cottage, unloading—all in cold weather, maybe snowstorms. She took a sip from her mug. "Yes. Let's be sensible and wait until spring. I'll tell Puddles." She added lightly, "Just being with you, my love, is a stay-at-home honeymoon."

He laughed.

As she went past him, with her free hand she rubbed his shoulder and he put his hand on hers. In her office she settled into the desk chair and reached for the phone, remembering how she and Bev had been bridesmaids at Puddles's wedding. Puddles, recovering from a hip replacement, wearing a plum dress and a rosy velvet jacket, had followed them down the church's aisle using a walker, in its basket her bridal bouquet of pink roses and miniature pink geraniums. Puddles's mother had been a geranium enthusiast.

Puddles answered the phone with her favorite Maine oath, "Son of a whore!" She continued, "I was just going to call *you*! I'm rereading one of my old Sue Barton nurse books, *Rural Nurse*. It's set in New Hampshire and I was getting homesick for my second home state."

"Happy New Year." This new year, Snowy thought, had to be happier than the awful year of 2008, awful except for marrying Tom and the arrival of Al. "Happy seventh anniversary as well."

"Seven years! And they said it wouldn't last!"

"Who said?"

"Well, nobody, but Aunt Izzy thought so for a spell before we tied the knot. I don't believe she really considered me a gold-digger. I think she feared it was too soon after Jill's death."

Jill was Blivit's first wife, who had met him while she was in college during her summer job working on a landscaping crew at his family's ice-cream company's tourist park. Like Puddles's first husband, Jill had died of a heart attack.

Puddles was saying, "We're having a nice quiet morning reading. In my *Rural Nurse*, there's a doozy of a mysterious typhoid epidemic going on, great fun. The book was published in nineteen-thirty-nine, the year you and I were born. *Rural Nurse* will be seventy years old this year, like us!"

"Unbelievable."

"Okay, speaking of marriage, when are you and Tom going to make a decision about your honeymoon?"

"We just did. What with the busy foliage season, the election, the problems with the Thetford store, and everything else, we've put it off too far, into the winter. You know how Tom feels the cold. We've decided we'd rather wait until spring."

"I've been betting with Blivit that you would."

Surprised, Snowy said, "You have?"

"'Failure to thrive,'" Puddles said.

This was the term Puddles had used for Tom's condition when he and Snowy had arrived in Maine in April; Puddles had explained that the term was used to describe undernourished children. Snowy said defensively, "He's thriving now, I've told you his doctors are pleased with his new knees, his progress—"

"But he'd thrive better on the island in springtime. Blivit of course thinks the island is wonderful in all seasons. Well, let's start getting definite about when you'll be here."

Snowy thought fast. "In May. Before things are hectic at the store from Memorial Day onward. Two weeks that will include his birthday, May fifteenth."

"It's a date! Oh, my God, in the new year how many years will it be since your first date with Tom?" Puddles called, "Blivit, what's nineteen-fifty-five from two thousand nine?"

Snowy heard Blivit say immediately, "Fifty-four."

"Fifty-four years," Puddles told Snowy. "Holy shit."

## 2. Snowy

Snowy replaced the receiver and stood up. The aroma of the stew was thickening the apartment's air. She went back into the living room and sang to Tom, "'Hey, good-lookin', whatcha got cookin'?'"

He grinned and reached for her.

They heard somebody knocking on the workshop's door.

She asked, "Who can that be? Have you unlocked it this morning?"

"Not yet." He started to get up. "Maybe David forgot his key, but he isn't working today."

"I'll go," she said, and hurried out the apartment door before he could protest.

Downstairs, the stew had seeped into the workshop's smell of sawdust and machinery. She opened the door and there stood Dudley and Charl, both similarly bundled up in parkas but Dudley tall, graying, balding, insouciant, and Charl small, brunette, apologetic, saying, "We should've phoned even if Ruhamah said it wasn't necessary."

Dudley announced, "We're on a Cheddar quest."

"Come in, come in." Snowy opened the door wide. Dudley and Charl had babysat Al at their Gunthwaite house last night so that Ruhamah and D. J. could go to a New Year's Eve party, and evidently these paternal grandparents had just returned him to his parents.

Charl sniffed. "You're having dinner, we're interrupting. Lamb?"

Upstairs, the stove timer began to buzz.

Snowy hugged her, then on tiptoe hugged Dudley. "Yes, lamb stew, but it's for supper, I'm cooking ahead. Come on up. Cheddar?"

Charl said, "Ruhamah told us you usually have some here so you wouldn't have to open up the store to get a piece for *somebody* who always wants some in the fridge even though he's watching his cholesterol."

"My fault," Dudley said. "I inadvertently ate our last chunk last night, without realizing there wasn't a backup."

Snowy said, "Your quest is over," and as she led the way up the stairs the buzzing stopped.

Tom was in the kitchen, raising the Dutch oven's lid. He said to Charl and Dudley, "Well, hello, and Happy New Year."

Snowy explained, "They've come to borrow a cup of sugar—oops, no, I mean a wedge of cheese."

Tom laughed and gave Charl a hug, shook hands with Dudley.

Snowy turned off the burner under the Dutch oven. Normally she would now add carrots, onions, and potatoes, but that could wait. "Would you like some coffee?"

Tom said, "Let me take your parkas."

Charl said, "Coffee would be nice," and unzipped her parka, revealing a brand-new-looking Fair Isle sweater above her jeans. A Christmas present. From Dudley or maybe from Darl, her twin? She unzipped her boots and stepped out of them. "I don't think I've relaxed since before Thanksgiving. Life gets so crazy during the holidays."

Dudley shrugged off his parka, in turn revealing a new-looking beige fleece sweater, and untied his boots and kicked them off. "Ruhamah told us you do mail-order cheese for summer people stranded without it in winter. Maybe I should put in an order, like Cheese-of-the-Month Club."

Charl said, "More like Cheese of the Week. Or Cheese of the Day."

Snowy took two Woodcombe General Store mugs out of a cupboard, poured coffee, remembered that Charl liked cream in hers despite cholesterol, and fetched a half-pint of half-and-half from the fridge. What to feed them? She grabbed napkins and onto a plate dumped the Walker's red package containing some shortbread left over from last night's dessert. "Let's sit down. How was Al's first New Year's Eve?"

"Rousing," Dudley said. "We whooped it up."

Charl sat down on the sofa, behind the coffee table still piled with Christmas cards from friends and relatives, the one from Ruhamah on top, showing the photo of Al and Ruhamah and D. J. "Dudley gave Al a lesson about presidents! Reciting all the U.S. presidents!"

Dudley sat down beside Charl. "When I got to Franklin Delano Roosevelt, Snowy, I told Al how you and I were in kindergarten on April twelfth, nineteen-forty-five, when the news reached the school that FDR had died. The teachers herded everybody outdoors to stand in front of the flag and say the Pledge of—the Pledge of—what's the word I want?"

"Allegiance," Snowy said, setting the plate and napkins on the coffee table. She looked hard at him, a worry nudging her.

"Allegiance," he repeated. "We said the Pledge of Allegiance."

Charl said, "After you got to President Obama, you told Al that one day his father will be added to the list of presidents. President Dudley Washburn Junior!"

Dudley munched shortbread.

Snowy sat down in the Martha Washington chair and Tom in his wing chair. A silence fell. In his youth, Dudley had planned to be president himself.

Tom asked, "How are things going in Gunthwaite?"

Snowy said, "How are your projects? The movie theater?" Several years ago, when the rundown movie theater on Main Street had been put up for sale, Dudley had organized a committee to figure out how the town could buy it, but negotiations were dragging on and on.

"What?" Dudley said. "Oh, it's taking even longer than I feared. As everyone always says, the devil is in the details."

Charl said, "Remember how we'd spend all our Saturday afternoons there? The double features? Darl and I would try to decide which actor was handsomest, Gregory Peck or Ronald Reagan or—"

"Speaking of presidents," Dudley said. Then he picked up Ruhamah's Christmas card, smiled at the photo, and picked up the card below. "May I?" He looked inside. "From George and Judy?"

Tom said, "My older brother and sister-in-law. Down in Florida."

Charl exclaimed, "Aren't they lucky!"

"Puddles and Blivit are back," Snowy said. "Back from South Carolina. I just phoned to wish them happy seventh anniversary." Charl and Dudley and Darl and her husband, Bill, had attended the wedding.

"Oh, their wedding!" Charl said. "In that darling church, and Puddles coming down the aisle with her walker, she was so brave! The flowers in the basket! Oh, flowers, that reminds me." She looked at her watch. "It's almost time for the Rose Parade on TV. Time to be on our way." She stood up and collected Dudley's mug and hers. "This has been fun."

Dudley got to his feet. "Let's not forget the cheese."

Snowy followed them into the kitchen and took the plastic-wrapped wedge of Cheddar out of the fridge and handed it to him. "*Bon appétit.*"

He asked, "Remember when FDR died and we went outdoors and said the Pledge of Allegiance?"

She looked at him. "Um, yes."

He looked back, as though waiting for her to say more. He didn't seem to realize he was repeating himself.

Now in her mind Yeats's words rampaged: Things-fall-apart-the-centre-cannot-hold.

Charl said, "Dudley, put on your boots." She hugged Snowy, then shoved her feet into her own boots, zipped them, snatched Dudley's parka and hers off the coat hooks. "Thanks so much. Don't bother coming with us downstairs."

Snowy hesitated. The phone began ringing. She checked the caller ID. "Bev," she told everyone.

Charl said, "Wish her Happy New Year from us. Bye!"

"I will. Bye." Snowy lifted the receiver. "Happy New Year, Bev, from us and from Charl and Dudley, they dropped in after returning Al—"

Bev said, "Roger wants us to move into the smallest bedroom so we can rent our bedroom at a higher price, I'm up here in it now, the master bedroom with the best view. We've got these three couples until Sunday and he's gone mad with greed, and I told him that if Pauline would go home we'd have that room to rent for a higher price, ground floor, its own entrance, but he said we need Pauline and she's a bargain." Bev finally paused. "The housecleaning, the breakfasts, I'm going to be *seventy* this year—Pauline made another new recipe, a New Year's Day breakfast strata this morning, that is, overnight, you know, it sits overnight in the fridge, and she got raves, she made it with raisin bread and apples and maple syrup and—" Bev screamed.

Snowy cried, "Bev, are you all right?"

"Alexis and Chad! Two of our guests! They just fell through the ice!"

## 3. Bev

BEV SHOVED THE PHONE INTO THE POCKET OF THE BERBER FLEECE vest she was wearing over her loon sweater and ran out of the bedroom, along the corridor, down the staircase, into the hallway. She shouted, "Roger!"

No answer.

She ran past the dining room and kitchen and banged on Pauline's door, calling, "Where's Roger?"

No answer.

Back to the kitchen, out the door onto the porch—and she heard Chad yelling, Alexis screaming. They had gone through the snow-covered ice a short distance from the shore, just beyond the water kept open around the dock by the agitator. The water wasn't deep there, yet it would be over their heads. Two ice-fishing bob houses stood farther out in the bay, but there weren't any vehicles or people fishing.

She had given all the winter guests the lecture she'd given her children and grandchildren: She didn't ever trust the ice, so she herself never went for a walk on the lake and neither should they. For the guests she'd added that if they felt they must, they should stay far away from that open water because naturally the ice would be thinner near it. Chad and Alexis either hadn't been listening or had believed they knew better than the locals.

The wind off the lake was slicing through her vest, her sweater, her corduroy pants. She grabbed the loop of rope and two life preservers hanging on the porch wall. Roger always claimed that the supply of life preservers and ropes in the boathouse was closer to the lake in an emergency, but she always insisted on having these, too. Back before Roger had moved in, back when she had first met Trulianne and Clem on the millennium's New Year's Day, she'd learned from Trulianne that Clem had fallen into the open water when toddling after an otter. Terrified, ever since then she'd kept life preservers and a rope where she could see them, the rope with a stone tied onto one end for weight. When Roger had noticed it during a visit he had scoffed, "You'll just knock the poor bastard out."

She needed Roger, she needed muscle. Running down the porch steps, no boots, just her socks and moccasins, she shouted again, "Roger!" She needed help. She remembered her phone and started to pull it out of her pocket.

"Roger?" Pauline leaned out the back door. "Bev, you don't have a coat on!"

"Call nine-one-one! Chad and Alexis have fallen in! Go find Roger, maybe he's in the garage!"

"Jesus, Mary, and Joseph." Pauline vanished.

Bev ran partway along the path Roger kept cleared with his snowblower, and then, breaking through the snow crust, she floundered down to a place on the banking opposite the hole in the ice, which widened as Chad and Alexis thrashed, treading water. She stood panting, scared. She couldn't throw the life preservers far enough, she knew she couldn't. If only she were Puddles, who had been the best pitcher in their softball games in gym classes!

She imagined herself Puddles and threw a life preserver. Chad lunged forward; ice cracked; he caught it, hung on, pushed it over to Alexis, who pulled herself up, parka sodden, to sprawl across it.

Bev threw the second life preserver. He caught it.

She checked the rope and shouted, "Be careful, there's a stone on the end!" She swung and threw the stone end, hanging on to the other. Chad caught it and passed it to Alexis, but Alexis didn't want to let go of her life preserver. He said something to her and then, lying across his life preserver, seemed to unpeel her grip and transfer her hands to the rope. Alexis's gloves looked very wet and cold, worse than Bev's own cold hands. Could Alexis hold on? Hypothermia! When did you start freezing to death?

Chad yelled, "Pull!"

Bev braced herself. And then Roger was suddenly smashing through snow behind her, in parka and boots so Pauline must've found him in the garage. He grabbed the rope from her and shouted to Alexis, "With your elbows, lift yourself up onto the ice!"

Bev stepped backward, out of the way.

Chad boosted Alexis onto the ice, and Roger drew her slowly toward the shore.

Now Pauline was hurrying down along the trodden snow, in her parka and boots, her arms holding blankets.

And right in the midst of all this in dead winter, Bev remembered a springtime party at a lakeside cottage after a junior prom, when a drunk Puddles on a raft had had to be rescued by Roger and Tom and swaddled in blankets. The lake, a constant in their lives.

Alexis reached the shore. Roger handed the rope to Bev and helped Alexis to her feet.

Pauline embraced Alexis with a blanket, saying "I called nine-one-one." She gave the other blanket to Roger for Chad and steered Alexis toward the house.

Roger took the rope back. "For God's sake, Bev, you go with them, you're freezing."

She realized she was indeed shivering, teeth chattering. "Be careful."

Her feet were so cold she could hardly bend them as she labored back to the porch steps and up to the door. Entering the house was like being put into an oven. She could hear, in Pauline's room, Dandy twittering, Alexis sobbing, and Pauline saying emphatically, "You're okay, your husband is okay, the ambulance will take you both to the hospital to make sure."

Bev collapsed into the kitchen rocker. Her hands were shaking, probably not only with cold. If she was in shock, what extreme version of this were Alexis and Chad in? She gingerly removed her socks and moccasins and massaged her stark white feet.

Pauline was telling Alexis, "Let's not waste time getting your clothes from the suite. You're too tall for anything of mine except this, one of my nice new flannel nightgowns, and here's my new bathrobe, and my feet are smaller but maybe my socks will fit—"

Bev stretched out her legs. Snowbanks had dampened her corduroys from the knees down. She padded into the laundry room, shut the door, stripped off the pants and threw them into the dryer. In the piles of folded laundry she located a pair of her socks. Also her green sweatshirt, so she swapped her cold vest and sweater for this. As she was pulling her pants back on, she noticed a pair of her slippers left here. She wouldn't have to drag herself upstairs to her closet for shoes.

Then she heard the ambulance in the driveway. She hurried into the corridor, meeting Alexis and Pauline. Despite dry clothes, Alexis was still shivering.

Bev said, "I'm so glad you're all right."

Alexis opened her mouth to reply. Closed it. Wordless.

They went out the front door onto the porch. Roger was talking to a guy, a paramedic.

Alexis screamed, "Where's Chad?"

Roger turned. "He's here, Alexis, he's already in the ambulance. Now you."

Pauline led Alexis to the paramedic.

Roger said to Alexis, "Phone us when you're being released and I'll come get you."

No reply.

The moment the ambulance swung off up the driveway, Roger ordered, "Indoors!" and herded Bev and Pauline into the house, down the corridor toward the kitchen. He said, "We need something hot to drink."

"Not for me," Pauline said. "I'm going back to my nap. That strata breakfast and then all this excitement have worn me out. Maybe I'm coming down with a cold."

"Eek!" Bev said. "Did you get your flu shot before—before you came here? We always get ours in October."

"I did. Now I just want to nap and listen to Dandy." Pauline proceeded to her room and Dandy.

In the kitchen, Roger wearily lowered himself into a chair at the table. Bev glanced at the loon clock and opened a cupboard. Almost noon; lunchtime; soup. She hadn't realized that Pauline napped, in the morning or afternoon. She'd assumed that Pauline always retired to her room to enjoy some private time with the magazines she got at the supermarket, what used to be called "women's magazines." Pauline also bought *People* magazine, and Bev admired her for knowing who the people in *People* were; nowadays, Bev knew hardly anybody except the British royals.

Roger said, "Let's hope the hell they don't sue us."

Bev swung around, clutching a can of Progresso Roasted Chicken Noodle. "Can they? Our insurance—and I gave them my lecture, you're a witness and so are our other guests."

"Let's hope they are embarrassed as well as relieved we saved them."

"If I hadn't happened to glance out a window . . . "

"That's how you saw what'd happened?"

"I was upstairs. You were in the garage?"

"Puttering."

Bev said, "We must give them a refund."

"And hope that word of their little adventure doesn't get from the hospital into the newspaper."

They stared at each other. How precarious, she thought, are our lives—and our livelihood; we should be wearing life preservers all the time.

"Lunch," she said. She dragged a saucepan out of another cupboard. She was too exhausted to make even a peanut-butter sandwich to go with the soup. They'd have crackers. Maybe, she thought, maybe this near-tragedy will distract him from his idea of renting their bedroom. But he was right, renting it would bring more money . . .

He said sardonically, "Happy New Year." He looked exhausted too. And when the loon clock erupted with its noon-time yodels, he didn't complain about her loons as he usually did.

# 4. Bev

In the following days, she hid from the Inn at East Bay by spending as much time at her Bide-a-Wee office as if this were one of the good years before the recession. She did actually receive two inquiries; she showed a condo and a house but nothing resulted. People were nervous. Within her own body, she felt the constant fluttering of panic. Panic about the future—and flashback panic: what if she hadn't glanced out the window and seen Alexis and Chad?

Otherwise, in her office she went through her files, hoping for inspiration about listings. She made notes for the summer theater's first planning meeting even though it wasn't until next month. And she read. It was going to be a long winter. One Wednesday afternoon she thought: *The Long Winter.* This was the title of the Laura Ingalls Wilder book she and Snowy had talked about rereading last winter; she hadn't got around to doing so. She phoned Mimi at the Thetford store and asked, "Am I interrupting? Are you busy?"

"Hi, Mother. Nope, there's an afternoon lull."

"Who has Laura Ingalls Wilder's *Long Winter*, you or Etta?"

"I've got it. I've got our whole series. During one of Etta's moves, she gave me those she had."

"I'm in the mood to reread it, to put this winter in perspective and remind me we're not starving to death."

"Yet," Mimi said, and laughed.

So Bev laughed. "Could you bring it to your store tomorrow and I'll come pick it up?"

"I could drop it off."

"I'd like to see your store. I've been meaning to. I haven't been to Thetford in ages." And by now, Bev hoped, she wouldn't start weeping at the sight of Mimi in a place of business that wasn't Weaverbird. "I'll be there tomorrow for your afternoon lull."

So the next afternoon she left Bide-a-Wee and drove north. The day was mostly sunny and the temperature had risen from this morning's five below zero. She thought of how her daughters had had a focus to their lives since childhood. For Mimi it was arts and crafts, particularly weaving. For Etta, horses. What, she thought, lay ahead for Abigail and Felicity, now that girls' futures seemed to have boundless possibilities, at least compared with the past?

Mimi at a general store, working for Snowy and Ruhamah.

Her own focus had come later in life, when she'd decided to take a real-estate course. If she couldn't keep up the mortgage payments on Bide-a-Wee, not only would that be the end of her business, but also Trulianne's and the roof over Trulianne's and Clem's heads.

Martin Luther King Day was this coming Monday, a long weekend for skiers. Roger had been revived by receiving three reservations again (none from Alexis and Chad!). She didn't know how she herself felt. She dreaded failure but she also dreaded success—oh, stop! This way lies madness! She and Roger were both relieved that Alexis and Chad's accident hadn't made it into the *Gunthwaite Herald*, at least. And she was relieved that so far he hadn't again mentioned moving out of the master bedroom.

*The Long Winter.* She suddenly remembered Snowy had mentioned that Puddles was rereading one of her old Sue Barton nurse books. Snowy had laughed and said she had an urge to reread one from her own youth, *Maida's Little Shop*, the first of the Maida series. Were they all in their second childhoods?

She turned off onto Thetford Road and approached the covered bridge. You were supposed to make a wish when you drove through. What to wish for? Recovery from the recession? Customers crowding into the office of Beverly Lambert, Realtor? Mimi's return to Weaverbird? Pauline's return to Greg? She said aloud, "I wish that Mimi's store will have good coffee."

She'd forgotten how pretty the village was, the waterfall splashing icy cold, the river and mountains, the white houses amid snowbanks. Pretty surroundings should help Mimi tolerate her job, shouldn't they?

The store's parking lot was empty. Bev parked and got out of the car, hoisting her shoulder bag. People did much longer commutes than Mimi, but still Mimi must be tired by the time she got home. Had Lloyd rallied enough to use his Crock-Pot skills for suppers?

Mimi opened the door. She was wearing a Thetford General Store sweatshirt. "I saw your car pull in."

Bev hugged her. "Isn't Thetford a pretty village!"

"Yes, it is." Mimi leaned back and looked her over. "You've recovered from rescuing that couple? You didn't catch a cold?"

"I'm fine. So is your father. Pauline didn't catch a cold either, and she thought she might already be coming down with one."

"You were heroic. The more I think about it, the more I know you were."

Snowy too had called her heroic when Bev had phoned to report that the guests had been rescued. Oh, horrors, now she *would* start weeping, because somebody besides Snowy had finally said "heroic." Not Roger. Bev hugged Mimi again. "I just did what everyone who lives on the lake ought to be prepared to do."

"Okay. Be modest. Let me take your parka. Would you like coffee? Cocoa?"

Bev unzipped her parka but kept it on. "Coffee would be lovely. I'll just stay for a quick cup."

Mimi led Bev over to the coffee counter and said, "At this time of day, I expect?" and lifted the carafe marked Decaf.

Bev had been planning a caffeine fix, but she nodded and turned to survey the store. Smaller than the Woodcombe General Store. Like Woodcombe's, it had a pickle barrel, a wheel of cheese under a glass dome, and a bulletin board. Without her glasses Bev could read the largest sign on the board, somebody offering his roof-shoveling services.

Mimi poured decaf into two Thetford General Store mugs. "We don't have scones like Cindy in Oakhill, but see, a Thetford woman makes hermits. Nice for dunking. Would you like one?"

Hermits: an old-fashioned hearty cookie, raisins, cinnamon, nutmeg. Bev wondered why these cookies were called that. If she'd ever known, she'd forgotten. How lucky real hermits were, living alone, not coping with people, making people's beds, emptying their wastebaskets. She said, "Thank you, Mimi, but no."

"I'm putting the recipe in Ruhamah's cookbook. How is Dad, really? How are reservations for this weekend? Here, sit down." Mimi went behind the checkout counter and pulled out a stool.

Bev set her shoulder bag on the counter, sat, and sipped. Good coffee; her wish had come true. "Three couples are coming again, not the couple who fell in the lake but the two other ones and Dudley and Charl's granddaughter and her husband, Lydia and Trent, who came at Thanksgiving. All skiers, but have you seen the forecasts? Tomorrow it'll be twenty below zero and thereabouts on Saturday, with a big snowstorm on Sunday, a foot and a half of snow. Your father thinks all three couples will call and cancel."

Mimi hooted. "Skiers? Dad should know better! He should remember how he'd speed from Connecticut up here to ski! They'll be in their element, skiing in a snowstorm. So you're getting return customers, that's a healthy sign."

"Well, Miranda and I will spend tomorrow readying everything in case they do come. And speaking of recipes, Pauline has found a recipe for pancakes made with cider, not milk, for lactose-intolerant Lydia, and she wants to try it Sunday. She's obviously never heard that rule about never trying new recipes on guests. She tests on our guests."

"Has she dropped any hints about being in touch with Kathy since the Christmas visit?"

"As a matter of fact," Bev said, "the other day a big carton arrived for her from Kathy, too big for our mailbox so the mailman brought it to the door. I tried not to look nosy and she lugged it off to her room, then later she mentioned that Kathy used to send her discarded magazines from Kathy's office waiting room and now Kathy has sent her a batch. Pauline likes magazines. It made me think of your great-grandparents, the CARE packages they sent Mother, worried that she was deprived of civilized reading in the wilds of New Hampshire. I wasn't much interested in the *New Yorker* and *Time* but I pored over *Life* magazine and the *Saturday Evening Post.* Anyway, maybe Pauline's latest recipes came from Kathy's magazines."

"Does Dad ever make any of the breakfasts, make his buttermilk pancakes?"

"No. His pancake performance was for you children. I'm going to make one of my tried-and-true recipes Saturday morning, my eggs Florentine."

"What about Lydia? There's cream cheese in your eggs Florentine."

"Lydia and Trent aren't getting here until Saturday afternoon. Hence the cider pancakes for her on Sunday. The others are due tomorrow afternoon or evening. *If* they decide to come. Pauline is planning Western omelets on Monday morning, cheese optional."

"Maybe you ought to do a cookbook too. Titled *Recipes from the Inn at East Bay*. It could be a little gift for guests."

Bev set down her mug. Was Mimi joking?

Mimi said, "Lloyd could design it. Ruhamah phoned and asked him about doing hers."

"Oh! Well, let's wait and see if the Inn at East Bay still exists after this winter. And keep waiting and hoping Etta's agent sells *her* book."

"All fingers and toes crossed, hoping."

Bev hesitated. "Mimi, are you okay? And Lloyd?"

"He has begun emerging. I guess that's how to put it. He's sort of started hunting for openings, but possibilities are few and they're downstate. We'd both have to commute—or else move." Mimi glanced out the window.

Two cars were pulling into the parking lot. Bev said, "The afternoon lull is over," and stood up.

Mimi reached under the counter and took out the old copy of *The Long Winter*. "A long winter indeed, and it's only January. Can you think about summer, look ahead to your summer theater?"

"The planning meeting is at the end of February. Auditions in March."

"*On Golden Pond*, will that be scheduled again? With you-know-who playing Ethel? You were so great."

Bev felt warmed, not just by coffee; Mimi thought she was heroic and a great Ethel. She confided, "Oh, it will be, Mimi. Last September, Russell—the director—told me that next year we'd end the season again with *On Golden Pond* and me."

Mimi hugged her.

Driving home, Bev switched on the radio and realized she was hearing a news bulletin. Oh, God, what now? A plane had crash-landed in the Hudson River!

# Chapter Five

# 1. Snowy

"HAVE YOU HEARD?" PATSY FLETCHER ASKED SNOWY, SETTING A quart of low-fat milk on the checkout counter. Patsy was always up on the news, local and worldwide. "In New York this afternoon, an airplane hit a flock of geese and the pilot landed safely in the Hudson River!"

"Wow," Snowy said, "that must've been quite a feat."

Patsy gave her a $5 bill. "Boats came right away and got everybody off. Nobody drowned, though I gather some were hurt."

Snowy made change, glad that Alan's death was so long ago Patsy didn't realize what she'd said. After a Fabulous Fifties party at Patsy and Nelson's house, Alan had stayed up when Snowy went to bed and then had driven to Woodcombe Lake with bottles of gin and Valium.

Patsy asked, "Ruhamah isn't here?"

"No, she and Al have gone home." Snowy checked the clock. Five-thirty, almost closing time. As usual when Al wasn't at Charl and Dudley's and came to work with Ruhamah, mother and son spent mealtimes in Snowy and Tom's apartment and went home early. Lately, Al had been here more often. Snowy thought: I must ask Ruhamah about Dudley, I must, I must. Why was this so difficult? Was she trying to preserve Dudley's—what, his dignity? And if she said "Alzheimer's" out loud to Ruhamah, dementia would be a reality.

"Nelson's Swedish meatballs recipe," Patsy said. "Could you tell her I corralled him to write it up today and I'll bring it in after I make a legible copy?"

Patsy had already brought her own recipe, macaroons. "I will. Thank you, Patsy." Snowy's cell phone rang in the pocket of her jeans.

"Bye!" Patsy said.

"Bye." Snowy slid out the phone and saw the caller ID: M. Hutchinson. Who? Blivit? He was Marcellus Hutchinson IV. But Puddles always did the phoning, not Blivit. Maybe for some reason Puddles was using Blivit's cell phone. "Hello?"

"Snowy?" Blivit's voice sounded taut.

Her heart began thudding with fear. "Blivit? Is everything okay?"

"Puddles is all right but there was an—accident at the high school, I mean, a wall collapsed, an inner wall of the cafeteria. We're at the Fort George hospital."

"Oh, no." Snowy remembered Tom's caustic prediction whenever he saw the Long Harbor High School: one of these days the goddamn thing is going to fall down.

Blivit blurted, "Sorry, I'm a bit, um, rattled, Puddles was working at the clinic and when the nine-one-one call was made and the clinic learned what had happened, she and Sheila—the PA—they took off to the school and got there first and went to work, seven kids injured but nobody killed. The ambulances arrived, and then Puddles tripped, she didn't see a chunk of debris. I was at my office, Sheila phoned me and told me what was happening, and when I got to the school the ambulances were busy, so I brought Puddles here to the hospital."

Fort George was the nearest city with a hospital. Puddles had had her hip replacement there. "She fell? Her hip—"

"It's not her hip, it's her right shoulder. She says it's broken, and you can imagine how furious at herself she is."

Snowy could.

Blivit rushed on, "I told her I'm phoning you but I'm not sure she listened. She's in the corridor seeing about the kids. We know them, of course, and their parents—she's bound and determined to help but she's only got one working arm, the left, she's right-handed—hell, you're well aware of that. If she can't be of help she wants to go home, she doesn't want to take up space here and wait around to get X-rayed, she's diagnosed herself, a clavicle fracture that doesn't need surgery, she won't admit she's in pain. I thought maybe you could talk sense to her. I'm sorry to bother you during store hours but—"

Snowy heard his desperate anxiety, his love. "Can you put her on the phone? I'll try."

"Hang on!"

Now there were other voices in the background, and then Puddles said, "Honest to God, this wasn't necessary. Blivit is the boy who cried wolf. If that's what I mean." And Puddles burst into tears.

"Puddles," Snowy said, "oh, Puddles."

"The kids. Eating their lunch, just kids having lunch. Kelly Wright, Brooke Bilodeau, Tori York, Andrew Elliott and Hunter Smith and Brady Conroy and Mason Sprague. Their blood. And me such a stupid klutz, tripping. Where's a damn Kleenex in this place? But I can't hold the phone and blow my damn nose, I can't one-handed, I'm such a klutz. Brady is from the island, concussion, fractures—and I can't help! So I might as well go home."

Snowy said, "Puddles, stay for the X-rays."

"I already know what it is, a clavicle fracture, and they'll just send me home. Immobilization, ibuprofen, icepacks—"

Voices interrupted.

Then Blivit said, "They've come to get her for the X-rays and she's going. I'm going with her. Thank you, Snowy."

"I didn't do anything!"

"I was prepared for her hip replacement but not for this, out of the blue. I'll keep you posted." Blivit disconnected.

Snowy stood listening to her heart thudding, then realized that the last customer, Ryan Hopkins, was watching her, his expression concerned. He held a boxed Paul Newman frozen pizza. A bachelor, Ryan had a home-services business, doing caretaking and plowing, and now he was heading to his own home with his supper.

He asked, "Bad news?"

"A friend fell and broke her shoulder."

"Ouch. Anyone I know?"

"She lives in Maine." Thinking aloud, Snowy added, "She's a nurse, but . . . "

He set the pizza on the counter. "Yeah. That could be a good thing and a bad thing."

"It could indeed."

From his wallet he extracted a $10 bill. "Hope she doesn't live alone like me. How'd I cook and eat my pizza with a shoulder out of commission?"

"Her husband," Snowy began, and stopped.

Ryan grinned. "Helpless?"

"Actually, he's a great cook, but . . . " As Snowy made change for Ryan, an idea began to swell.

After he left, she immediately phoned Ruhamah.

"Hi," Ruhamah said. "Everything under control?"

"No. I've had a phone call from Blivit. There's been an accident at the high school, some students were hurt, and Puddles fell and broke her shoulder. Blivit sounds thrown for a loop. I'm thinking I should go help, maybe stay a week."

Without missing a beat, Ruhamah said, "Of course you should. Invite yourself and bring Tom. Not your honeymoon, but even if you're staying in their house and not in Cotter Cottage you'll be at the ocean."

"That's what's dawning on me. But can you and Rita handle things?"

"Yes. It's winter. And there's always Leon to fill in if necessary."

Leon had in the past. Another of Bev's children working for us, Snowy thought. "When I get to the apartment I'll phone Blivit and then let you know his reaction. If it's a yes, I'll have to spend tomorrow organizing and packing so we can drive there Saturday before Sunday's storm."

"I'll tell Rita. Don't worry about anything except Puddles."

"Okay. Thank you, my baby," Snowy said, using the old endearment she still could use even though Ruhamah had a baby herself now.

She pulled on her parka, swapped her shoes for her boots, locked up, and went outdoors into the evening, cold and shadowy. As she hurried along the street, she dreaded the cold in tomorrow's forecast, twenty below. Could she really get organized and packed tomorrow? Last year she had taken a carful of stuff to Maine, but most of that had been supplies for island-living, so wouldn't this be a lot easier?

Her mind kept leapfrogging over the bigger question: Would Tom balk and say no? Tom possessed that Scottish characteristic called thrawn, which could be summed up as: ornery. If a Scot is told to do something, he will do the opposite.

Another idea occurred to her. On the evening after the New Year's Day talk with Puddles about May honeymooning, she had conferred with Tom and written Mildred Cotter about renting the cottage. She hadn't yet heard back. She intended to try phoning if she didn't hear by February, but maybe on their way they could stop at the Portland rehab place and see her and thus have news for Puddles about a real honeymoon on the island.

But don't suggest that until—*if*—they were on their way.

She reached the barn and went in. Tom and David had also closed up shop for the day. She climbed the stairs and found Tom in the kitchen readying supper, on the counter a can of Campbell's French Onion Soup, a can of tomato paste, and a bottle of Worcestershire sauce, with a skillet on an unlit stove burner. Tonight's meal would be an old favorite from his mother's repertoire, Salisbury Steak. The salt content was sky-high but that was part of the nostalgia. She said, "Tom, your prediction came true," and as she took off her parka and boots she told him about Blivit's phone call. Then she crossed the kitchen and put her arms around him.

He said, "Poor Puddles."

Into his flannel shirt, his solid chest, she said, "Blivit is coming unglued."

"He must be thinking it's his fault even though he wasn't on the school board when they and the town voted to save money and have the shop teacher design the new school. Fucking idiots."

She lifted her head and looked up at Tom. "He's on the school board now. He's been chairman how many years?"

"Building codes weren't followed."

"Puddles always says that Long Harbor can be kind of like the Wild West, way at the end of the peninsula. Lawless, on occasion."

"Well," Tom said, letting go of her, "there'll be lawsuits."

Oh, God, Snowy thought. Before Puddles and Blivit had met, a Long Harbor cheerleader had been killed doing a stunt. The lawsuit lasted years. She said, "Yes, but right now the main thing for us is Puddles. And Blivit coping with Puddles." Tom didn't reply. She plunged on, "They need help. They need us. We've stayed with them often, and we've always had a standing invitation to come anytime. Let's do it now. We can be useful—and also see the ocean."

He turned back to the counter and yanked the tabs off the cans of soup and tomato paste. Then he said, "She's got her daughters. One of them's a doctor, for God's sake. They should be the people helping."

"They have jobs. Careers. In South Carolina."

"How about her father and his, um, girlfriend?"

"Mr. Pond is ninety-two and Ginny is eighty-nine."

"What about Aunt Izzy, nearby on the island?"

"She's eighty-seven."

"Well, there's the housekeeper."

"Tammy," Snowy said. "She'll help, and so will other Long Harbor folks, but—" She didn't know what else to say. She said, "Puddles has been my dear friend ever since she arrived in eighth grade and the homeroom teacher told me to take care of her."

"Shit," Tom said. He went to the refrigerator and yanked out a package of ground beef. "Shit shit shit."

Snowy gathered that this meant yes. Decision made, and now she was scared by it. She said, "I'll phone Blivit."

## 2. Snowy

Whirlwind honeymoon, Snowy thought on Saturday morning as she and Tom drove out of Woodcombe, Tom at the wheel of the Subaru. Or at least whirlwind packing. They hadn't had a whirlwind courtship if you counted as courtship all the years before her proposal and their wedding, but yesterday's organizing and packing had definitely been whirlwindy, and in the back of the car was the result. David had arrived for their departure and helped them load the luggage: their big suitcase, her vanity case, and Woodcombe General Store tote bags filled with extras like hiking boots, fleece caps, and plastic-wrapped packages of the store's fudge and Cheddar. On the back seat, protected by the car's emergency blanket, were her laptop and, in case she got a chance to do some writing work, her briefcase packed with a legal pad, a pen and pencil, and the folder containing copies of her latest poems.

What, she wondered, have I forgotten to bring? And how will I, not a nurse, attempt to take care of Nurse Puddles?

The morning was sunny, the temperature higher than yesterday's, today a tropical sixteen below zero, and the car's heater made the interior snug. Last April, Tom had been almost completely silent during their drive to Long Harbor. He was silent now, too. Was he remembering that drive?

Up out of the Woodcombe valley, to the main road heading east.

Tom spoke. "When we're coming home, we'll be surprised to see mountains on the horizon instead of ocean."

Relieved, she said, "Good old New Hampshire mountains. Meanwhile, the ocean!" She decided to sing. Often they had sung on their trips, but not last year. "'A capital ship,'" she sang, "'for an ocean trip was the Walloping Window Blind.'"

He joined in. And after they finished the saga of the ship, the road continued leading them toward the coast.

When she had phoned Blivit Thursday evening, he sounded as if he'd reached the end of his rope, saying, "Thanks for calling back, we're home but she won't go to bed early, I'll put her on." Snowy had said, "Wait a second, please, Blivit. Tom and I would like to come visit and help out, and we can arrive Saturday and stay a week, would that be all right?" He said fervently, "Oh, my God, yes." When Puddles took the phone, Snowy said, "We're coming Saturday for a visit." Puddles asked suspiciously, "To look after me?" "To see the ocean," Snowy said, "and incidentally you and Blivit." "Ha," Puddles said, "it's not necessary, but if it gets you to Long Harbor, fine." Then Snowy phoned Bev and told her what had happened. Bev seemed distracted by preparations for the Martin Luther King weekend guests, but she said, "Give her hugs from me, eek, her shoulder, you can't! Give her my love, oodles and oodles of love."

At nearly the last minute, as they neared the exit to the bypass around Portland, Snowy finally said to Tom, "Let's stop and visit Mildred."

"Mildred? Mildred Cotter?"

"Let's drop in at her rehab place."

"We can't just drop in. When we saw her last year, she knew we were coming."

"We can ask at the desk. Those treats I brought for Puddles and Blivit, we could give one package of fudge to Mildred or, if we can't see her, leave it for her. With a note about renting the cottage, to remind her about my letter."

After a pause, to her astonishment he said, "Okay."

He drove into the Portland suburbs, and at the end of a residential street they approached the Pines Manor Rehabilitation and Retirement Center.

Not much snow here. The vast leach field, the first sight that welcomed you, was an expanse of dead brown grass edged with white snow, matching the white plastic vent pipes. The driveway curved toward a small parking lot in front of a lengthy three-story white clapboard building.

Tom parked, and they got out of the car, Tom stretching his legs, Snowy her aching back. The morning was somewhat warmer in Portland but nonetheless the cold hit hard.

He asked, "Do I hear barking?"

Yes, she heard it coming from indoors. "Four-legged visitors, maybe?"

"Or maybe the owners kicked out the oldsters and turned it into an animal home. You wanted fudge?" He opened the car's hatch.

She reached in and took one of the packages out of a tote bag. "All set."

The barking became louder as they went up the front stairs, and when Tom opened the door the noise was a canine cacophony of octaves—squeaks, yapping, basso profundo.

Last year when they had entered the building into this lobby, she'd thought it felt like a big hotel, with maroon wall-to-wall carpeting and a polished reception desk. It still did, and the same young woman was at the desk. No dogs visible. But today the receptionist wasn't sitting down and she didn't look smoothly professional; she was standing, gripping the edge of the desk, and seemed to be trying to catch her breath.

Snowy raised her voice over the din. "Hello, we're friends of Mildred Cotter—"

The receptionist gasped, "Here comes another one!"

A small black puppy scooted into the lobby, pursued by a panting middle-aged woman. The puppy veered toward Snowy, perhaps his keen nose attracted by the fudge.

Tom laughed and grabbed him. Snowy remembered how, on her sixteenth birthday, Tom had picked up her barking Sheltie and said, "Calm down, pups," and Laurie had immediately subsided. Tom had said, "Dogs like me. So do old ladies." Now her seventieth birthday was looming and she would truly be an old lady who liked Tom.

The middle-aged woman gasped, "Thank you!" She surveyed Tom holding the puppy. "I'm Jane and this mischievous cockapoo is Pepper. Would you like to adopt him and give him a 'forever home'?"

Tom said, "I'm already the grandfather of a chocolate Lab named Swiss Miss."

Who belonged to Tom's granddaughter Lilac.

Jane smiled at him, took Pepper out of his arms, and explained, "Today is dog-therapy day at the Pines, and I'm one of the volunteers at the local shelter. We bring doggy sunshine to the senior citizens."

The receptionist pointed down the hall. "Mildred is with the others in the community room."

Snowy said, "Maybe I'd better leave this fudge here for Mildred," and set the package on the desk.

The receptionist looked at it warily, as if it might attract the Hound of the Baskervilles. Jane led the way to a room where last time Snowy had glimpsed people at the tables working on jigsaw puzzles or playing cards. Now, dogs and puppies were dodging around the tables and chairs and wheelchairs and walkers, while people sat patting some, settling some on their laps, the old folks' faces getting ecstatically licked.

Sitting hemmed in by her walker, Mildred held a little white fluffy dog, a sight that surprised Snowy. Indeed, she realized she was surprised that Mildred was even attending a dog-therapy session. Although a pretty old lady, in an aqua sweater adorned with appliquéd pink posies, her navy slacks crisp, Mildred certainly wasn't a sweet old lady and Snowy would've thought her impervious to dogs' charms. Mildred glanced up from the dog, saw Snowy and Tom and then said to the dog, "Well, look what the cat dragged in."

Tom laughed.

Snowy babbled, "We're on our way to visit Blivit and Puddles and just stopped by to say hello—"

"Hello," Mildred said. "This is Fifi. Or so Jane tells me."

At the moment, Jane was letting Pepper loose again into the rampage.

Mildred continued, "You just stopped by to see if I got your letter. I did, but I'm planning to be back in my cottage in May."

"Oh," Snowy said blankly.

Mildred patted Fifi.

Tom said, "Well, that's good news, that you're on the mend. And the cottage will help more. I've realized how much Cotter Cottage got me on the mend last year after my knee replacements. Thank you for that."

All at once Snowy's eyes filled.

If Mildred noticed, she didn't comment. She stopped patting Fifi and stared at Tom.

He took Snowy's arm and added, "Our best wishes to you," and steered Snowy out of the room.

The receptionist asked, "You found Mildred?"

"Yes," Tom said, "and we had a brief chat. Good luck with Pepper and the rest of the kennel." He hurried Snowy out the front door into the cold, down the stairs, across the parking lot to the car. Opening the passenger door for her, he said, "It'll be all right, Blivit will find us some other cottage."

"Then—then you want to go in May anyway?"

"Another cottage might be better." He hesitated. "No memories, no associations."

So, his contentment at the end of their stay hadn't obliterated the memory of his misery at the outset. They got into the car. She pulled Kleenex out of her shoulder bag and dabbed at her eyes as she remembered the cottage bedroom's blue-painted slant-top desk in front of a bedroom window, the desk she'd grown so fond of while she worked there with the ocean view, sometimes putting on her hiking cap to shade her face when the sun grew hot.

He reached over, patted her knee. As if she were Fifi? "It'll be all right, Snowy."

She couldn't help saying, "Mildred hasn't progressed from using a walker. How can she manage at the cottage? Wishful thinking?"

"Probably. But enough to outweigh the thousand dollars we'd pay." He started the car. "Next stop, Moody's Diner for lunch."

She roused herself from the desk memory and said, "Onward!"

Moody's Diner in Waldoboro was a landmark and stopping there a tradition in Bev's family that had begun with Bev's parents' honeymoon. Bev had introduced Snowy to the place when they drove to Maine for a get-together with Puddles in Camden, and since then Snowy and Tom had developed their own tradition on trips to Long Harbor. But last year he'd hardly spoken during the meal and he hadn't wanted dessert. This year, unwinding in their booth, they talked, speculating about the care of Puddles, and after their traditional crabmeat rolls he said, "Dessert?" and they both ordered Moody's famous walnut pie.

Usually they'd swapped drivers after Moody's, but last year they hadn't because Tom seemed to be hell-bent on proving he could drive the entire distance with his new knees. This year as they went outdoors she asked, "Shall I take over?"

"Sure," he said.

The next landmark came in Camden. She always pointed out the Whitehall Inn as they went past even though he knew all about this important place. She and Bev and Puddles had spent a night here, the very inn where young Edna St. Vincent Millay had recited "Renascence." This year Snowy said, "Living inland. After growing up here, she ended up living inland. Upstate New York with her husband. Dying there."

"Are you thinking you're lucky to have spent most of your life in the Lakes Region where you were born?"

Startled, she looked over at him. "Do you think you are?"

"Is it our 'forever home'?"

She sought an answer. He began to sing "The Walloping Window Blind" again, and she joined in. And then as they kept on along Route 1, they commented on sights, in Lincolnville saying they should take a ferry out to Islesboro sometime, in Belfast saying they should spend a day here sometime, in Searsport saying they should stop and visit the Penobscot Marine Museum sometime. Finally they came to the turnoff down Perkins Peninsula, and she drove through blueberry barrens smeared with snow, to Long Harbor. She checked the dashboard clock. Four-thirty, close enough to the estimated time of arrival she'd given Blivit.

At the top of the hill above the town, she slowed in front of the high school. Trucks were parked every which way in the parking lot, their lettering identifying contractors, electricians, carpenters. Working on the weekend.

"Jesus H. Christ," Tom said. "What a royal fuckup. Well, the kids who didn't get hurt must be happy; I bet the school will be closed for quite a while."

The school-activity sign on the white lawn announced that tonight the Long Harbor High School Seafarers would be playing a basketball game at the Clarendon High School. Snowy said, "That sign. Was this how it was scheduled or have they switched it to Clarendon from this gym? Or have they canceled it and not changed the sign? If it's on, Puddles will be champing at the bit to be with her cheerleaders."

"Does she have an assistant?"

"She got one of their mothers to help during her hip replacement."

He said, "The school will have the game, saying that the injured kids would want them to go ahead." He drove down the hill clustered with houses.

Usually when they neared the waterfront Main Street she opened her window to see and smell the ocean, but nope, on this cold day she kept it closed, like the gift shops and art galleries and most of the restaurants with wintertime bleak boarded-up fronts. However, Leander's Lobster Pound and the Seaview Café were open as usual and for once their signs didn't compete with slogans but proclaimed the same thing: Our Prayers Are With You. Snowy glanced down Grove Street at the Long Harbor Family Health Center, a white clapboard house from which Puddles and the PA had dashed to the rescue.

Then she turned onto Creamery Point and drove past the big white Quarry Island Ice Cream building, which Puddles always said looked like the Taj Mahal. It and the cute ice-cream parlor were open. Around it in the Quarry Island Ice Cream Park the snow-covered grounds were empty, there were no cows in the pasture, and the various attractions were closed until spring, the gift shop, the arts-and-crafts gallery, the farm museum; no band was playing Golden Oldies on the bandstand. Another turn, onto Blivit's little gravel private road. The gatehouse wasn't used in the winter and the gate bar was lifted. The road continued on through the woods, becoming a driveway after another empty pasture. All the cows must be in the gray-shingled barn, where they were tended by Blivit's farmer. The driveway led to the large white saltwater farmhouse, and she could see the ocean behind it.

The moment she stopped the car, Blivit opened the front door as if he'd been watching for them, a big man with receding gray hair, rimless glasses, wearing his usual L.L.Bean winter attire, flannel shirt, fleece vest, and corduroys.

She scrambled out of the car as fast as her back would allow. "Hi, we're here, we're in Maine at last!"

"Snowy, Tom." Blivit hastened down the stairs, hugged her, shook Tom's hand. "Come help me talk Puddles out of going to a basketball game tonight."

## 3. Bev

PAULINE SNAPPED, "*FERME TA BOUCHE!*"

Loading the dishwasher with the Sunday breakfast dishes, Bev recoiled. Then she almost laughed. Pauline sounded just like Marie, her mother, who in moments of stress reverted to French, including the admonition to *shut your mouth.* But when Pauline had announced she was going to have a nap, Bev had merely asked if she was getting overtired here and maybe needed to take it easier with the inn's duties. Exercising restraint, Bev had not suggested a return to Greg.

Pauline continued, "It's normal to be tired! I've been standing over the stove making one million damn pancakes!" She marched out of the kitchen.

Bev straightened up and adjusted her black ski sweater she was wearing today in honor of their skiing guests. She hadn't worn it for actual skiing since last year, when she'd gone with Roger and Mimi and Lloyd to the Gunthwaite ski area; Roger alone used the slopes, while she and her daughter and son-in-law had a calmer time on the cross-country trail. She poked the dishwasher's Start button. Out the kitchen windows the scene was white; the snowstorm had started early this morning, and the lake was hazy, the mountains gone. But as Mimi had predicted, the weather forecast hadn't discouraged the guests. All three couples had arrived and now in all three cars were driving over to the ski area.

The ice was getting close around the dock's pilings; in this far-below-zero cold, the agitator was just barely keeping it away. There was that worry as well as the worry about the cost of the furnace coming on constantly in the cold—and the worry of a power outage (as the electricity company liked to call it instead of a power failure) and what if the generator again didn't respond?

Supposedly worry-free, the guests were off playing. And Roger had been playing with his truck's plow, clearing the driveway so the guests could reach the road and go play. First he'd shoveled the front stairs and a path to the garage. Now he was probably tinkering with the snowblower before clearing longer paths. Not really clearing, not with the snow still falling; he called it keeping up with the storm. And, be honest, she told herself, he wasn't really playing.

*Pauline* claimed to be tired? I'm worn to a frazzle, Bev thought. She always liked to quote her own mother, so she said aloud, "I've been running around like a chicken with its head cut off," an expression Mother had used once in a great while. Because Bev had been born on a chicken farm—well, actually in the Gunthwaite hospital but brought home to the farm—she always felt she could use this expression too, even though she'd never seen such a sight, thank God. But Mother had.

Then she thought: Honestly and seriously, am I physically able to do this work? Snowy claimed that admitting to limitations was one of the hardest parts of aging. If the inn didn't fail and actually did begin to make a profit, could she keep going? Could Roger?

She almost switched on the kitchen TV and sat down for a rest. The Sunday programs would be about the inauguration of President Obama tomorrow and that would be happy news.

No. She had to tidy the dining room. Then she had to check the bedrooms to make sure nobody had left a hair dryer on or done something else that might cause a disaster.

So she took the hand vacuum and dustpan and Swiffer duster out of the broom closet. As she went into the dining room she reminded herself once again that she should buy one of those crumb pans called a silent butler, which probably meant searching antiques stores. Silent? She needed a *living* butler! She needed Jeeves to help polish Mother's silver candlesticks on the dining table, the silver pepper mill, the silver platter under the centerpiece she'd chosen for this weekend, a carving of a crouched skier that Roger had bought some years ago at a League of New Hampshire Craftsmen shop. The carving had a title carved into its base: “Over the Headwall.” This was the headwall that skiers loved in Tuckerman Ravine on Mount Washington, and Roger had often talked about attempting to ski down it but he’d never been that foolhardy.

Mother had woven the seats for the six dining-room chairs. On the sideboard, an amaryllis was blooming the lush crimson shown on the bulb’s package, a color Bev had bought to go with the red beach ball in the painting of “Waterlight in Summertime” that hung over the sideboard, done by Harriet. When Grace and Walter, the retired couple who’d been here at New Year’s and were now en route to the Gunthwaite slopes, had had their first breakfast here, Grace had studied Harriet’s signature in the painting’s corner and asked, “*The* Harriet Blumburg?” As Bev later told Snowy, “I impressed her even more by saying Harriet was my best friend’s college roommate. So satisfying!”

She shook the place mats woven by Mimi, brushed crumbs into the dustpan, dusted the table, replaced the place mats, and vacuumed up crumbs on the Oriental rug. In the kitchen, she emptied the dustpan into the wastebasket. No, she would not sit down and watch a Sunday program.

First, the Loon Suite, again Lydia and Trent’s choice. She went down the corridor past the living room, where yesterday she’d set out the board games that were usually stored in a window seat. Nobody had used any, yet.

It was foolish to feel like an intruder when she checked rooms; the inn was *her* house, Waterlight had been her dream house. But as she took the master key out of a pocket in her jeans, she was assailed by guilt—and by anger at having to do this task.

She remembered the excitement of matching customers to their dream houses. She remembered being unfettered and free, driving to look at places to list, driving people to see them. So many lives she'd changed by showing people the houses they wanted or didn't realize they wanted!

Was she getting desperate enough to start behaving like a real-estate agent in the Inn on East Bay? She'd thought from the beginning that the guests must be just guests, not potential customers harassed with sales pitches, and she was just their hostess, making gracious small talk. Also their cook and housekeeper and everything else, tending to their every need. Innkeepers, Roger had read, had to be caregivers.

Unfettered. An inn trapped you, just as the general store trapped Snowy.

Maybe she could put a little stack of her business cards on the desk in the hallway. Was even that too obvious, too crass, for her principles? Would Roger object? What were his principles?

On the desk in the suite's sitting room, Lydia and Trent had set their matching Mac laptops. A phone rang and, startled, Bev jumped, then realized it was her cell phone. She yanked it out of her jeans. From Snowy! "Hi, Snowy, are you in Maine?"

## 4. Bev

"YES," SNOWY SAID, "WE GOT HERE YESTERDAY AFTERNOON ON schedule."

"How is Puddles?"

"Well . . . "

Bev sat down at the desk. "She's being a handful?"

"A left-handful! Her right arm is in a sling and she's trying to learn to be a leftie and not succeeding, at least not yet."

"Where are you calling from, your guest room?" At Puddles's house, Snowy's room was the downstairs guest room, evidently because of the safety rail that had been installed in its private bathroom's shower when Puddles was recuperating after her hip replacement and had stayed in this bedroom, unable to climb to her and Blivit's bedroom. Puddles had diagnosed Snowy's scoliosis before any doctor had, and she decreed that Snowy should have a safety rail. Bev always got an upstairs guest room and a shared bathroom, which theoretically should make her feel less old and decrepit than Snowy. The upstairs room was nice, featuring the ocean view, a seagrass rug, and bed linen patterned with crustaceans.

Snowy said, "Yes, we're in 'my' room, our room, and Tom's reading a *Down East* magazine."

Bev pictured Snowy and Tom together in the room, probably sitting in its two armchairs. Snowy and Tom seemed to blend. She saw herself and Roger as so separate, even when they were whooping it up in bed.

Snowy was saying, "Puddles is propped up with cushions on the living-room sofa with her cell phone in that left hand, talking to Amy. Susan called earlier. Puddles called them both Thursday evening and they've been calling back since, making sure they're not needed."

Amy was the doctor-daughter; Susan, her twin, owned Puddles's first husband's construction business. Bev said, "I bet they're extremely relieved you're there. How's Blivit doing?"

"This morning he escaped to his lab. Sunday can be his day of rest there. But he's awfully upset and brooding. He feels responsible for the condition of the high school and—well, anyway, Tom and I are getting an outing tomorrow. Puddles wants us to take her to the Fort George hospital to visit the kids. She says she's up to it and she reminds us that she's the nurse. So we're not arguing."

"Then the injured students are all—recovering?"

"The only one in Intensive Care has been moved to a regular room."

"It's awful, Snowy. What's that phrase of Harriet's you told me about, for 'there are no words'?"

"*Ein milim.*"

"*Ein milim,*" Bev repeated, standing up and walking into the suite's bedroom. She looked out the windows. "The storm is supposed to end mid-afternoon here, with a foot of snow or more. How's your weather?"

"We're not supposed to get that much. Are your guests off skiing?"

"Heading there right now." Bev suddenly remembered some news she hadn't dared tell Snowy because Snowy hated snowmobiles. But maybe it'd be comic relief, amusing relief. "Speaking of winter sports, guess what. This fall, Jim Milford, you know, the manager of Gunthwaite Hardware, brought his snowmobile to Trulianne's for her to get it ready for winter, the way he usually does, but *this year* he's divorced. And lo and behold, earlier this month Trulianne dropped a hint about her private life! I'd asked something-or-other about a weekend and she said she and Clem had gone snowmobiling with Jim. His snowmobile is big enough for passengers. Is it a budding romance on a Ski-Doo?"

Snowy didn't laugh. She sputtered, "Amid pollution, noise and air pollution! Terrifying the animals!"

Eek, not funny to Snowy. On the bedside tables on either side of the bed were Lydia's and Trent's bedtime reading. Endearingly, Lydia's (Bev assumed) was *Selected Poems* by Henrietta Snow. Using her own left hand, Bev lifted the cover and peeked. Snowy had inscribed it to Charl and Dudley, so Lydia must have borrowed the book when she and Trent stopped in at her grandparents' on their way here yesterday. Trent's book was a history of the World War II ski patrol, the 10th Mountain Division.

Snowy had recovered from the snowmobile news and was saying, "Puddles phoned her father Thursday evening, too. Mr. Pond and Ginny are sweeties, they've sent flowers."

"I thought of doing that but I got sidetracked. Snowy, I'm checking the rooms now and I just discovered Lydia's reading material. A copy of your *Selected Poems*!" No need for Snowy to know that Lydia had borrowed it, not bought it.

Snowy exclaimed, "Isn't she also a sweetie!" Then she said, "Tammy is here, helping out even on a Sunday—hey, look, Tom, we have a visitor—hello, Puffin, welcome."

Puffin, Puddles's latest cat, must've entered the guest room. Bev cooed, "Hi, Puffin."

"Which reminds me," Snowy said. "Cats and dogs. On our way here, we stopped at Mildred Cotter's rehab place, and it was visiting day for a riot of dogs from a shelter. We—" She paused.

Bev looked into the bathroom. The hair dryer was unplugged. As she had seen when checking rooms at Thanksgiving, Lydia's choice in lotions and lip balm was Burt's Bees.

Snowy continued, her voice sad, "Remember, I told you I'd written her about renting her cottage this year and hadn't heard back? So we asked her. She said no. She thinks she's capable of returning there, but we doubt it, and so do Blivit and Puddles."

"Oh, damn, Snowy, you loved that place."

"Blivit says that either he or Aunt Izzy will find us another cottage for our May honeymoon." Snowy's voice became determinedly cheerful. "Meanwhile, Aunt Izzy phoned me and invited Tom and me to the castle if we need a respite from Puddles, though Aunt Izzy didn't put it quite that way. She referred to Puddles as 'poor child,' as in, 'Merciful heavens, the poor child with a broken shoulder!' Do you think maybe later Puddles will appreciate learning that from Aunt Izzy's vantage point she's a child? I told her we'd better stay here with Puddles."

"How is Puddles doing?"

"She's blustering, but . . . More than her shoulder seems broken. Maybe her . . . "

Bev tried to find the words. "Her spirit?"

"Yes."

"Poor, poor Puddles."

A silence, in which Bev heard Tom ask, "Can we interpret Puffin's stare? Does it mean he's hungry and Puddles and Tammy are ignoring him or is he just curious?"

Snowy said to Tom, "Blivit fed him breakfast." To Bev she said, "Well, I'd better go find out if Puffin gets elevenses."

"Thank you for calling, Snowy. Give Puddles my love."

But instead of saying good-bye, Snowy asked, "How are you bearing up, taking care of all those people this long weekend?"

Bev said lightly, "I'm planning to count how many weeks there are until Presidents' Day weekend and hope we don't get any guests in between, though I know I should be hoping for guests every weekend, even every weekday." But then she added, "When the children were young—you only had Ruhamah, not my passel, but still, did you ever think, 'I can't do this anymore, it's not what I imagined, I can't keep on'?"

After a moment Snowy said, "Come along, Puffin, we're going to go ask Puddles what you want. Tom, you're all set until we make lunch?"

Bev heard Tom say, quoting one of Puddles's Maine expressions, "I'm as happy as a clam at high tide."

Then, evidently out of their room and out of earshot, Snowy said to Bev, "For me, that happened last year. With Tom's reaction to the knee replacements, the oxycodone, the depression. So I took him to the ocean."

"Oh. Yes."

"Is there any way you can leave Waterlight, let Roger and Pauline run it, and come here after we leave? Tell them Puddles needs you?"

"Does she?"

"I guess I won't know until our week is drawing to a close."

"I can't, Snowy. I'm still trying to run a real-estate business too." Bev heard a bellow. Roger was yelling her name. Oh, horrors, what now? "Again, thanks for the update and give Puddles my love. Bye."

She hurried out of the suite and down the corridor. Roger stood in the hallway looking like the Abominable Snowman in his snow-soaked parka, jeans, boots, and knit cap, his mustache frosty or snotty or both. He reeked of fuel fumes.

He said, "The goddamn snowblower wouldn't start! Then it did and I began and then it kept cutting out. And then it stopped altogether. Phone Leon and tell him to get over here with his and clear the paths."

# Chapter Six

# 1. Snowy

Snowy looked out the Subaru's windshield at Fort George, a port city she and Tom hadn't visited before. The morning seemed to be faltering into sunshine after the storm, making the snowbanks glow white. Tom was driving, and Puddles was in the backseat giving directions although the H-for-hospital street signs were clear enough, leading them to a Main Street of spiffed-up brick buildings and then to a wide street where houses that looked like ship captains' homes had become doctors' offices and probably some had been razed for parking lots.

"There it is," Puddles said. "Don't take the entrance road with the Emergency sign. We want the next one."

But Tom did slow down briefly at that sign. Probably, Snowy thought, he was thinking of the ambulances arriving from Long Harbor last Thursday, as she and certainly Puddles were. The next entrance widened into a big parking lot cramped by the freshly plowed snow piles and already crowded with cars. Beyond stood the hospital. What must be the original brick building had been extended by a conglomeration of wings and even a flying buttress. Still, it was much smaller than Dartmouth-Hitchcock Medical Center, where Tom had had his knees replaced, and there was no real resemblance, yet as Tom drove around searching for a parking space, Snowy suddenly feared the memories. But at least she and Tom didn't have to enter the hospital. Puddles had declared that she would do the visiting on her own while they went sightseeing.

Puddles said, "There's one, grab it!"

Tom parked and dashed around the car to Puddles's door, which she was struggling to open left-handed. He opened it, joking, "At your service, madam."

Puddles asked, "How the hell am I going to learn to be a southpaw if you won't let me try?" But she allowed him to help her out.

And this morning she had allowed Snowy to help her get dolled up for the hospital visit in her mauve cashmere twinset (appropriate for the mother of twins), black knit slacks, black suede ankle boots. Earlier in Snowy and Tom's visit, Puddles had decided that earrings were too tricky for Snowy to insert into her pierced ears—"You'll stab me!"—so she wore none, but today she allowed Snowy to fasten a necklace. Snowy had been intrigued by the necklace Puddles chose, one Snowy hadn't seen before, a silver chain with a black onyx pendant. When Snowy inquired about it, Puddles had said, "A present from Blivit. Onyx is the seventh-anniversary gem, but I didn't know that for my first seventh anniversary," and then she'd caressed it and actually blushed. Her sling didn't fit into her color scheme, being navy blue. Over her outfit she was wearing her best coat, gray lambswool, the right sleeve empty.

Snowy got out of the car into a strong wind that blew her unzipped parka open. "A sea breeze," she told herself aloud, clutching the parka tight, and asked Puddles, "Are you positive you wouldn't like us to come in with you?"

"Absolutely positively positive." Puddles adjusted her black shoulder bag on her left shoulder, a shoulder bag's usual place for right-handed women, and looked at her nurse's watch, on the usual left wrist. "Okay, almost ten. Go say hi to the ocean and see the lighthouse. Keep on down this street, onto the main road. As I told you, the lighthouse is closed off-season but the view isn't. Then get yourselves a seafood lunch. Off-season, I recommend Main Street's Fort George Diner. I'll meet you at the reception desk at two o'clock." She started toward the hotel entrance.

Tom said, "Wait up, Puddles. Before, you said we'd stop for lunch on the way home. Two o'clock means four hours of seeing the kids. Isn't that too much? I thought we were talking about a couple of hours, until noon."

Puddles glowered. "I'll be fine."

Tom pointed out, "You're supposed to be taking things easy, not to mention a daily afternoon nap."

"I knew you'd say that," said Puddles.

Snowy asked, "What about your own lunch?"

"I'll get something in the hospital cafeteria. I like hospital cafeterias."

Snowy turned to Tom, mutely asking what to do.

He said firmly to Puddles, sounding like the teacher he used to be, "We'll return here at noon and take you to lunch en route home." Then he grinned and added, "That was the schedule in my mind and, as Pooh says, I am a bear of very little brain. So let's stick to my schedule."

Puddles looked startled and perhaps disarmed by the introduction of Winnie-the-Pooh into the argument. "Okay. But meet me in the cafeteria. We'll have lunch there."

If she thought she would scare them off with hospital food, she didn't succeed. Tom laughed. "Okay, the cafeteria at noon."

Snowy bade farewell to the scallops she'd been planning to order at whatever restaurant they stopped at on their drive back to Long Harbor. Well, Blivit had been serving seafood suppers, his lobster pot pie on Saturday night and his tomato-topped baked haddock last night, so she could hope for scallops tonight. Dear Blivit!

Puddles said, "See you later, alligator," and again started across the parking lot.

Snowy replied, "Toodle-oo, kangaroo."

She and Tom watched Puddles walk away. The sea breeze pushed Puddles's empty coat sleeve in a backward wave and an automatic door ushered her into the hospital.

"Well," Tom said. "Did I win a battle but lose the war?"

"You were wonderful."

"Sure. I'm freezing, let's get back in the car and find the lighthouse." But he stood there a moment longer. "Would it be better therapy just to let her do what she wants to do?"

"We pretty much have. Such as staying up with her and her DVD collection of *M*A*S*H*."

"So Blivit can go to bed." He opened the passenger door, and she got in. He went around the car and slid behind the steering wheel and added, "Puddles hasn't said a word about retiring. This would be her opportunity to retire from nursing or coaching or both."

Snowy looked at him. "I'm sure it hasn't even entered her mind." But retirement had entered Tom's mind.

He drove out of the parking lot and along the street of more homes renovated into something else, then onto a road on which various stores offered, amongst other merchandise, discount furniture, marine supplies, and Italians (meaning Italian sandwiches). Gradually the roadside emptied of everything but spruces. Then, after several miles, all at once around a bend a great blue bay opened up.

Snowy gasped but didn't speak and neither did Tom.

The wind was whipping here, the spruces swaying. It had blown any snow off the road's verges, revealing buff-colored grasses flattened by its force. The road curved up and up a headland. She felt as if she were in an airplane taking off, lifting over the bay.

Around a final curve they saw lighthouse signs and a parking lot in front of a white house with a red roof. Beyond the house, a long walkway stretched to the lighthouse itself, not one of the tall lighthouses but squat, black above white brick. It resembled a giant peppermill.

This thought made her think of Pepper the cockapoo and the nursing home and Mildred—and the gone-forever Cotter Cottage.

Tom drove into the parking lot. "I wonder if we can see Quarry Island from up here. Puddles didn't mention that."

"Let's find out." She zipped her parka.

He kept his gloves in the glove compartment, lined leather gloves. Also his tam. While he put these on, she found her fleece gloves in her shoulder bag. With all her strength, she shoved open her door.

Out of the car, they bent into the wind and walked to the white house's sign. It told them that this had been the lightkeeper's house and was now a museum and would be open from Memorial Day through Columbus Day.

Tom said, "We can come back if our honeymoon includes Memorial Day."

Up the walkway they climbed, Snowy hanging on to the railing, until they reached the railing-enclosed bare brown lawn of the lighthouse.

"Damn," he said. "Didn't think to pack binoculars or borrow a pair."

Snowy squinted. There were patches of islands in the distance but they looked too flat, without Quarry Island's distinctive silhouette rising to Hutchinson Mountain. "Is the angle wrong? Are we looking due east? Quarry Island would be northeast of Fort George."

"I'm guessing we're looking Down East."

"So we can't see it from here."

But they could practically see Spain.

And, adjusted to the wind, they stayed looking longer than she ever thought they could when they'd got out of the car. While she looked, at first she concentrated on the ocean's swelling and dipping, but then this mindfulness shattered into a kaleidoscope of thoughts: Tom had loosened up here even with the Puddles worries and might he continue more relaxed at home; was David being completely honest when earlier this month she'd pulled him aside for a chat and he told her Tom was letting him handle more of the heavy work; the fire tower; owning three general stores during the nation's economic mess; should she be worrying about Dudley's capabilities when he and Charl were taking care of Al; she *must* talk to Ruhamah about Dudley; what was that funny-sounding term for a landscaped view, maybe "terminal vista"; would there be a snowstorm on the evening she was scheduled to do a reading next month at the Midhurst library downstate; was Ruhamah working too much after her store hours, coping with plans for the cookbook and the anniversary party? The cookbook! Her own main contribution to the cookbook would be copy editing and proofreading, and what mistakes might she miss? Just spelling "sesquicentennial" was a challenge!

Food. Next Sunday was Burns Night, when she would as usual make Cock-a-Leekie Soup for supper. Sometimes for dessert she made the oatmeal-and-whisky trifle called cranachan, but last year she'd only opened a packet of Walker's shortbread. This year she would make cranachan.

Ah, food. Would a port-city hospital perhaps have fresh seafood?

This last detour of her mind made her check her watch. "We'd better start back, if we're not frozen solid."

In the car he immediately switched on the ignition and twisted the heater dial to high. Then he sighed what sounded like a happy sigh and said, "Let's take Aunt Izzy up on her invitation later this week. On Thursday, we could catch the morning ferry to the island. Come back on Friday, head home Saturday."

Snowy leaned across the console and kissed him.

After a while he said, "Speaking of solid. But not frozen."

She laughed. "Going parking . . . "

He drove back to the hospital, where in the lobby they followed signs and other visitors to an elevator down to the cafeteria and the aroma of hamburgers and fish chowder. This big room was sort of an above-ground basement. The normal-size windows showed leafless shrubbery and an area that must be a patio in patio weather. Patients' families were wandering around seeking comfort food, while doctors and nurses in scrubs briskly collected their lunch items. The array of offerings both dazzled and dismayed her. Nourishment for the families, yes, but no real comfort under these circumstances. Yet such a lot of work for the cafeteria staff, the short-order cooking, the sandwich-making, a salad bar, a coffee bar, and across the room the refrigerators' glass doors displaying already-made sandwiches and clear plastic containers of individual desserts—and there she spotted Puddles, coat awry, awkwardly opening a fridge left-handed and reaching for one of those containers.

Snowy nudged Tom and pointed. They hurried across the room.

Puddles dropped the container, which held a slice of chocolate cake with thick chocolate frosting.

"Got it," Tom said, picking the container up.

Puddles snatched it back. "I should get a cookie, easier for a leftie to eat, but I want chocolate cake."

A chocolate fix. Snowy stopped herself from asking if the cake was all that Puddles planned to dine on. Instead she asked, "How are the kids?"

Puddles shot back, "How do you think they are?" She turned toward the cashier at the checkout counter. "You get your lunches, I'll get a table."

Tom pulled out his wallet and tucked a $5 bill under Puddles's thumb on the container. "So you don't have to wrestle with your pocketbook." He drew Snowy toward the soup counter. "Fish chowder. What do you want to bet the fish is fresh?"

Their tray became filled with two bowls of chowder, two packets of crackers, two mugs of coffee—no, three—and two slices of apple pie, plus plastic utensils and napkins. Snowy paid the cashier. Tom carried the tray to the table at which Puddles sat slumped, watching a nearby table of nurses talking and laughing. She hadn't opened the cake container—or hadn't been able to. He set Puddles's mug in front of her and opened the container. She didn't comment.

Snowy and Tom sat and ate chowder. Right out of the ocean and off the docks.

Puddles said, "I'm not used to being taken care of. With the hip, I could plan for that. But this? It's supposed to be the other way around. I'm not used to being a visitor at a patient's bedside. I'm supposed to be the nurse."

Snowy nodded, and Tom said, "We know."

Puddles reached for her mug. "A few years ago I got to thinking that kids, instead of being more vulnerable, were tougher than older people because they didn't know what life could do. Now these kids do. As the kids in the school shootings know." She took a gulp of coffee and sat up straight. "I talked with Brady Conroy, the boy from the island, and he told me that Aunt Izzy had visited him and the other kids yesterday. When she phoned us Saturday, she'd told Blivit she planned to come in from the island with Emily, and now she has."

Emily, a carefree young woman, was Aunt Izzy's helper and the granddaughter of Aunt Izzy's best friend. Snowy said, "I hope that was therapeutic for everyone."

"Well," Puddles said. "Yes, I suppose." She took another gulp. "Okay, you two. After that phone call, Blivit let it slip that Aunt Izzy told him she was inviting you out to the island. A pre-honeymoon. For God's sake, *go*."

## 2. Snowy

THURSDAY WAS MURKY AND THE TEMPERATURE 20°, SO WHEN AT 7 a.m. Snowy and Tom boarded the Uncle Sam, the mail-boat ferry, she didn't consider sitting on the deck to avoid seasickness. In the deckhouse they sat on a bench near the propane heater. The only other passengers were a married couple about their age; the husband explained that he was coming home after a heart attack and three stents; the wife sitting close to him was quiet, exhausted. Yesterday at the Long Harbor grocery store Snowy had bought a piece of gingerroot to forestall seasickness but she left it in her parka pocket, not gnawing it like a nervous landlubber, and she got through the forty-five-minute ride without disgracing herself either way.

In the cold vapor the Quarry Island harbor and village looked ethereal, a dream come true. The harbor was nearly empty, the lobster boats and the castle boat put up for the winter. On the public dock Aunt Izzy stood waiting for them. She hadn't sent Emily to meet them; she'd come herself. She wore a heavy parka, her white curls defying a pulled-down navy watch cap, her jeans displaying their plaid flannel lining by their perky turned-up cuffs. She spoke to the couple and hugged them before springing forward to hug Snowy and say to Tom as she hugged him, "I can't resist a handsome man!"

Tom laughed.

The little parking lot held only a few cars, including Aunt Izzy's old Volvo station wagon. After Tom stowed the single suitcase they'd brought here, she invited Snowy to sit up front in the passenger seat and then said as she drove sedately onto the main road, "Let's stop at the school. I told Amber you were coming for an overnight visit and she invited us to drop in and say hello."

Snowy asked, "Amber is still here?" Amber was the young one-room-schoolhouse teacher, and last April Aunt Izzy had figured that Amber's first winter on the island had been quite enough for her.

"Yes," said Aunt Izzy. "She surprised us with her stamina. The students remember you, Tom. Of course Chloe and Lily, the eighth-graders with whom you discussed *My Antonia*, are going to the Long Harbor High School now. Trevor, the seventh-grader with whom you discussed *Treasure Island*, is now the one and only eighth-grader."

Snowy glanced over her shoulder at Tom. He was leaning forward, head swiveling, looking out windows at the winter scenery they remembered from that cold New Year's Day wedding. Less snow than on the mainland. The island not Vacationland (the slogan on Maine license plates) but isolated, an outpost on the ocean. The familiar village, its stark general store, the tiny post office, the granite town hall.

He asked, "How many kids in all at the school this year?"

"Seven," Aunt Izzy said. "As we feared, one of the new families couldn't adapt to island life, so they and their two children left. Needless to say, my great-grandchildren are still here, Priscilla in kindergarten, Christopher in second grade." She continued past the church and stopped in the schoolyard.

The white clapboard school seemed gray in this weather, but the windows were staring intently with bright electric light. Aunt Izzy sprang out of the car before Tom could open her door and led the way up the walk to the front door. He did manage to reach around her to open that.

Aunt Izzy said to Snowy, "Handsome, and such a gentleman!"

The chilly hallway smelled of winter clothes, the parkas hanging on pegs and the boots beneath. Aunt Izzy knocked on the schoolroom door, opened it, and asked, "May we interrupt?"

Ponytail swaying, Amber rose from her teacher's desk near the propane heater at the front of the room. She looked happier and more self-possessed than last year. Snowy wondered if Aunt Izzy had discreetly not explained that Amber's decision to stay was caused by a budding romance with a young lobsterman. Then she chided herself: You're always the romantic, but don't go—er—overboard.

"Isabella," Amber said, "do come in. Hello, Tom, Snowy." To the students she said, "Let's say, 'Welcome!'"

From their desks they chorused, "Welcome!," with Priscilla and Christopher waving at Aunt Izzy.

The room's warmth was also welcoming. Snowy watched Tom taking it all in, the traditional decorations of snowflakes cut from paper doilies, some math on the chalkboard, on the bulletin board a photo of Martin Luther King Jr. delivering his "I Have a Dream" speech, a bookcase full of tall and regular books, and out the windows the ocean.

"Hi, Trevor," Tom said to the oldest kid. "How's it going?"

Amber said, "Trevor, why don't you tell Tom some of the novels you've been reading lately."

Trevor stood up. "Hi, Tom. I've read *Robinson Crusoe* and *David Copperfield*, and now I'm reading *The Old Man and the Sea*."

Amber said to Snowy, "As I explained to Tom last year, we intersperse the sea stories."

Trevor said, "Next it's *Oliver Twist*. I prefer Hemingway to Dickens."

Tom hesitated, then remarked, "For an interesting insight into Hemingway's writing, you could look up what he said a writer should have. I can't quote it here because there's a four-letter word—" He looked questioningly at Amber.

She said dryly, "I know the quote, Tom, and I don't think any of us would faint, not even the little ones. Or Isabella."

So Tom said, "Hemingway observed that 'the most essential gift for a good writer is a built-in shockproof shit detector.'"

A startled beat of silence, then laughter.

Aunt Izzy said, "An excellent exit line. Bye now!"

They left, and outdoors Tom said, "Last year I learned how liberating it is to be a volunteer, not an employed teacher."

Back behind the Volvo's wheel, Aunt Izzy returned to the road and announced, "Here's my suggestion for the rest of your day. After you unpack and freshen up, why don't you take this car—or Blivit's island Jeep you used last year, it's in the carriage house—and get reacquainted with the island. Emily will pack you a picnic lunch to eat in the vehicle. And I have a surprise. I've located a cottage for your honeymoon."

Snowy spun around to look at Tom, looked back at Aunt Izzy, and exclaimed, "A cottage? You've already found us a cottage? Aunt Izzy, you're a wonder!"

"A final phone call last evening. On your drive around the island, you can stop and see it, from the outside at least. I don't yet have the key. Next," continued Aunt Izzy, "supper tonight. Florence and Roddy"—her granddaughter and grandson-in-law—"will be coming to see you, bringing Christopher and Priscilla. I checked with Blivit and he hasn't given you his oyster stew yet, so Emily and I will give you ours."

And thus their day was planned. After Aunt Izzy drove past the castle's gatehouse and between the granite gateposts topped with granite urns of evergreens and up to the granite castle's rambunctious collection of architectural styles, turrets and towers and a red tile roof, she led them into the great hall and said, "You are in the blue room, as on past visits. When you're ready for the picnic hamper, you'll find us in the kitchen."

Snowy and Tom climbed the carved stone staircase to the second floor and the bedroom whose bed had a canopy of blue silk and whose armchairs were upholstered in morning glories. She took off her parka, visited the room's blue-toweled bathroom, hung tomorrow's clothes in the closet, and then she and Tom went back downstairs. From the hall they made their way to the kitchen and voices, Aunt Izzy and Emily chatting amid the glass-fronted cupboards, the soapstone sinks. The kitchen had a butler's pantry, and next-door was the servants' dining room from the days of yore when the castle employed thirty people; now it was used as extra space for meal preparation. Emily hugged them and handed Tom a cooler (not a hamper), saying, "Salmon-salad sandwiches."

Tom said, "Thank you, a favorite," and Snowy said, "Yum."

Aunt Izzy held up two sets of keys. "Volvo or Jeep?"

As Snowy had expected, Tom said, "Jeep, please."

Aunt Izzy gave Snowy a torn-off page from a memo pad bordered with seagulls. "I hardly need to write down the directions to the cottage, but I did. Just go on along the road to South Harbor and it's the first driveway after the fish houses. The Morris family has been spending summers here for a hundred years, arriving on the Fourth of July. They've never rented it before, but I—prevailed. The cost is the same as Mildred was charging you. We'll work out the details as May draws nigh."

Snowy and Tom said in unison, "Thank you."

As they walked to the granite carriage house, Tom laughed and said, "'Prevailed'!"

In the Jeep Wagoneer they drove out between the gateposts and south along this road they'd taken during their daily drives last year. It followed the shore for a while before changing its mind and curving into spruces. Tom braked as a thin deer bounded across the road. The deer population was too big for the island, but winter lowered it with hardships Snowy tried not to think about.

South Harbor, at the bottom tip of the island, had waves splashing frothy on rocks and a view of smaller islands' silhouettes on the horizon. Beyond the lobstermen's fish houses, which were shacks festooned with multi-colored lobster buoys, a narrow driveway descended to—*the* cottage! She gaped at the exact type of cottage she'd imagined last year when she'd asked Puddles to find a place on Quarry Island. It was a Cape whose shingles had turned silver with age. White clapboard ells had been added later. Under the snow she knew there must be the wild roses, *rosa rugosa*, she'd imagined. In May they wouldn't yet be blooming and pouring forth their pink fragrance too fragile to be cloying, but she would be breathing them anyway.

Suddenly she noticed a small driftwood sign over the front door. It told her the name of the cottage: Sea-Fever.

"My God," she said, "look, look, 'Sea-Fever'! Is it a coincidence or did they deliberately choose the title of that John

Masefield poem, 'I must go down to the seas again, to the lonely sea and the sky'?"

Tom reached into the back for the cooler. "Let's have our picnic early." He took out two cans of Moxie. "Here's to our honeymoon!"

## 3. Bev

THERE WERE THREE WEEKS BETWEEN MARTIN LUTHER KING DAY weekend and Presidents' Day weekend, and Bev's hopes that no guests would come were dashed each week. The weekend of January 24th, the Inn at East Bay had three reservations, for the Loon Suite, Heron, and Merganser. The next week, another foot of snow fell, and the inn was full that weekend, with skiers in the Loon Suite, Heron, Merganser, and Wood Duck. Bev feared Roger might say he would rent the master bedroom and pitch a tent on a snowbank in which he and she could sleep; he didn't, but he scribbled more than ever on his legal pad. The weekend of February 7th brought guests to Heron, Merganser, and Wood Duck. This year, Presidents' Day weekend included Valentine's Day on Saturday, and the inn was full again.

The strain of the work seemed to compress her body. No time to catch her breath, not even on a weekday when she could escape to her office. The Wednesday afternoon after Presidents' Day weekend she fled, driving to Bide-a-Wee choking with guilt because she should still be up to her elbows in housework with Miranda and Pauline but frantic to find some real-estate connection she'd missed, some way to link a house and a house-seeker. As she got out of her car, she heard Trulianne clanging away inside the workshop. Clem wasn't home from school yet. She collected the mail from the office's roadside mailbox and took it indoors where she defiantly went to the Keurig machine and made herself a cup of caffeinated coffee. Yes, caffeine in the afternoon *and* made with Keurig's expensive thingamajigs she should be saving for customers. Who would not come. At her lovely desk she looked around her lovely office, at the lovely curtains Mimi had woven. She put on her glasses, skimmed the mail, all junk, and then just sat here, a failed realtor.

Might the inn actually become a success—or at least a way to survive? Could she and Roger survive making it a success?

As of today, his birthday, he was seventy-two years old. They'd arranged with the children that there would be no big celebration on a weekday birthday when everybody was working, but Dick and his family sent him a birthday card, as did Mimi and Lloyd, Leon and Clem, Etta and Steve and Jeremy. Mimi and Etta had insisted she take Roger out for a birthday dinner tonight so she wouldn't have to cook. Usually she made him her seafood casserole and his favorite cake, coconut, though in recent years she'd bought the cake at Indulgences—

Her cell phone rang. Caller ID said it was Mimi, phoning during her workday.

"Hi," Bev said. "Is everything all right?"

"Yes, it's the Thetford afternoon lull."

But Mimi didn't sound lulled. Bev said, "I'm at the office. I, um, had to check things."

Mimi said, "Lloyd has become obsessed with Mrs. Pollifax."

Oh, my God. "Who?"

"When Lloyd was at the dump a couple of weeks ago, he was browsing in the Swap Shop, you know, where people leave free things too good to throw out, and he brought some paperbacks home. One of them was a Mrs. Pollifax. It's a series. Have you read it?"

"No."

"I'd read the first one a long time ago, she's a widow who is hired by the CIA in a mix-up and she goes off to foreign countries spying and solving mysteries. Lloyd got hooked. He's bought the whole damn series from Amazon and gone back and started at the beginning. I think he's hiding, in denial again, not emerging, not even attempting to job-hunt anymore, just taking some freelance stuff that comes in like Ruhamah's cookbook. Mostly he reads Mrs. Pollifax. He's never read any mysteries before. If Etta's book gets published, I would've expected him not to read it—or only so he'd know what we'll all be talking about."

Etta's book. Which Snowy was concealing. Then Bev remembered that last year Snowy had told her she'd noticed Mildred Cotter's collection of Mary Stewart's novels at Cotter Cottage, had begun rereading them there, and had continued with library books when she returned to Woodcombe. Had Snowy been hiding? Or had she been reviving, getting her strength back after the worries about Tom? Bev asked Mimi, "Is Lloyd's reading called binge-reading?"

"Whatever it is, it's exasperating. No, it's more than exasperating, it's scary."

Bev heard a door in Thetford open and close.

Mimi said, "A customer. Have you and Dad decided where you're going to dinner?"

"He says he doesn't want to bother changing clothes or getting all dressed up so we'll go to Hooper's."

"Oh, like a high-school date. It'll be a belated Valentine's Day as well as a birthday. How romantic!"

Bev doubted Roger had thought of this. He was probably thinking of saving money, especially with Hooper's senior-citizen section of the menu. Well, they'd both been too busy last Saturday to pay attention to Valentine's Day; she'd mention it to him at Hooper's. "Mimi," she said, "maybe Lloyd isn't hiding. Maybe he's still sort of healing from the shock of Leicester Printing's closing."

"Gotta go. Give Dad a birthday hug from me."

"Bye, darling." After tapping the phone off, Bev touched and smoothed her desk's surface, picturing Mimi's Weaverbird shop bereft of Mimi. Should she herself relinquish this office? Before Roger suggested it again? She finished her coffee, growing cold.

And then she returned to Waterlight to join Miranda and Pauline.

Roger didn't want to dine fashionably late, either. At 5 p.m. he came into the laundry room where she was folding the last batch of sheets and said, "Let's go."

"Okay." She checked her appearance in the full-length mirror, an old magenta sweater and old jeans, and remembered getting dressed up for dates that included Hooper's. Should she at least run upstairs to her jewelry box and put on the little gold basketball on a gold chain that Roger had given her when they started going steady? But he was in a hurry. She followed him into the corridor. Miranda had already left, and from the sounds in the television room Pauline had as usual collapsed with a glass of merlot and the New Hampshire early evening news. "I'll tell Pauline we're leaving."

"No need," Roger said.

But Bev did anyway, hurrying on and leaning into the television room. "We're off, Pauline."

"Off like a herd of turtles," said Pauline. "Or like Greg used to say, 'Off like a turd of hurtles.'"

Bev laughed and joined Roger at the hallway closet, where he helped her on with her parka. She said, "Pauline just quoted a little saying of Greg's. Maybe that's a good sign?"

"A good sign of what?"

Bev sighed. Roger opened the front door. The evening was darkening. Winter. She thought of the Ingalls family's *Long Winter* she'd reread last month. Maybe she should binge-read the Little House series.

They crossed the porch and went down the stairs to her car. Roger got into the driver's seat. Up the driveway and along Lakeside Road he drove, past the closed cottages, into town, into alive neighborhoods, to Main Street and its neon lights. She tried to resurrect in her mind the Main Street places that were gone or changed, Sweetland Restaurant, Woolworth's, the shoe store where she and Snowy had bought their first pairs of heels, the Rexall drugstore, the original Yvonne's Apparel dress shop, the fruit store with its drive-in theater placards getting flyspecked in its windows.

Years ago, Hooper's Dairy Bar had expanded into Hooper's Family Restaurant. But the owners had had the sense to keep the original horseshoe-shaped counter, and after she and Roger walked past the counter and a waitress led them to a booth in the added-on wing, Bev looked back at it and imagined their teenage selves sitting there. From Hooper's, on dates, they would go parking on the Cat Path. Oh, their hot-and-bothered young love!

The waitress asked, "What can I get you to drink?"

When Hooper's became a family restaurant, it acquired a liquor license. Did being a parent mean that you needed more sustenance than a Coke? Instead of ordering iced tea as usual, Bev said, "A glass of chardonnay, please."

Roger deliberated. Usually he had a cup of coffee with meals here. Now, even on his birthday, was he counting the extra expense of booze? If he ordered from the senior-citizen section, the price of a meal was a dollar less and included coffee, also a scoop of ice cream for dessert. He said, "I guess I'll have a Bud Light."

"You got it," the waitress said, and departed.

Bev opened her menu, though she could recite everything on it except the Daily Specials on the inserted page. She usually had the grilled chicken Caesar salad, dressing on the side. She should have something different and fattening tonight. Throw caution to the wind and live it up!

His menu unopened, Roger was gazing out the window at Main Street. "Snowstorm tomorrow."

"I'll go to the cemetery on Friday instead." Sixty-four years ago tomorrow, on February 19, 1945, the assault on Iwo Jima had begun. Daddy had been killed in the third wave. Since her return to Gunthwaite, she had visited his grave in Birchwood Cemetery on the 19th, adjusting the date to the weather if necessary. She added, "Yesterday I had an e-mail from Snowy worrying about the weather for a reading she's supposed to do at the Midhurst library Thursday evening."

"She'll have to cancel."

"Yes." Would Snowy be relieved? Bev knew that Snowy still suffered from stage fright.

The waitress brought their drinks. "Are you ready to order?"

Bev said, "I'd like one of your Wednesday specials. The Chicken Alfredo, please."

Roger said, "I'll have the senior-citizen version of the pot-roast dinner."

"You got it," the waitress said, and departed again.

Roger said, "These snowstorms certainly have been good for business. Full up again this coming weekend. If it carries over into spring and summer, I'm thinking we could become an events venue."

Bev stared at him. "A what?"

"We could host weddings, things like that."

Bev wanted to give up, to put her head down on the table and weep and give up. She felt Mimi prodding her and lifted her wineglass. "Happy birthday!"

He didn't lift his beer glass. "Seventy-two years old. Hard to believe."

Still holding her wineglass aloft, she blurted, "Mimi pointed out that this could be a Valentine's Day celebration, too, since we didn't have time on Saturday. And actually, it's an anniversary. When I was a sophomore and you were a senior, the Friday before Valentine's Day there was a basketball game that night and a dance afterward and then we went parking on the Cat Path and you asked me to go steady and gave me your little gold basketball. Remember?"

"Whom were we playing?"

"Playing?"

"What school? Who won?"

"I don't remember." She added, still trying, "Snowy might."

"Yes, she was a cheerleader." He finally lifted his beer glass and clinked it against her wineglass. "And you were a leading lady."

Taken aback, flustered, she laughed and made her Marilyn Monroe face at him, dropping her eyelids and pouting her lips.

He said, "If business stays this good into the summer, you're not going to have time for the summer theater."

His words hit her, sickened her, and she feared she might vomit.

Taking a swig of beer, he returned to gazing out the window.

They sat in silence.

## 4. Bev

*DRIVING MISS DAISY*, BEV THOUGHT, HANGING LOON TOWELS IN the Loon Suite's bathroom on Friday afternoon for Russell's son and daughter-in-law due tomorrow. Russell, her director. Last week he'd phoned her to make the reservation for them, and during the small talk he'd mentioned that at the summer theater's planning meeting next week he would announce doing *Driving Miss Daisy* this season. He didn't say she'd be Miss Daisy, but her hopes had been high.

Again she heard Roger's warning, "You're not going to have time for the summer theater," and again her stomach lurched. She had managed not to throw up in Hooper's and she must not throw up here in the nice clean toilet.

Yesterday's snowstorm had been one of the pretty storms, bringing sticky flakes that coated every twig and limb in every tree, creating thick white scenery. The snow had continued into early morning today, eight inches of it, and now Roger had finished plowing the driveway and was clearing the paths with his repaired snowblower and his shovel. At the moment he was snowblowing; she could hear the racket even inside the house.

Men had heart attacks shoveling. Even while snowblowing, men dropped dead.

Was she hoping he would? Frightening herself, she made a mental note to insist to him that Leon at least do the shoveling. Insist? Roger would ignore her.

She hurried out of the Loon Suite. She'd already told Miranda, who was busy upstairs, that she'd be going to the cemetery. Pauline had left for the mall right after Roger got the driveway plowed, her errands including last-minute shopping for the weekend.

Bev stopped stock-still. She had suddenly pictured Leon's bedroom in the Connecticut house. As she had long ago confessed to Snowy and Puddles, she'd sort of snooped in her children's rooms, worried about teenagers and drugs. And sure enough, in fourteen-year-old Leon's room, in the toe of a revolting sneaker, she'd found a Baggie of marijuana. She hadn't told Roger. She'd sat Leon down for a talk. And then, becoming cowardly, she'd never checked his room thoroughly again.

Wondering why she was doing this, she walked down the hall to the shut door of the Grebe Room. Pauline's room. She tried the door. It was unlocked. So she could snoop. She pushed the door farther open, reminding herself that Dandy was a canary, not a parrot who might tattle. And Dandy in his cage on the stand was a welcome sight, homey and slightly messy amid the surroundings of a bedroom so spic-and-span that she was reminded of the old Gunthwaite term she'd almost forgotten, "nasty-neat French." The stack of magazines on the table beside the armchair was as tidily arranged as if this were still a B-and-B room.

Bev tiptoed to the closet. Yes, Pauline's new clothes hung aligned beautifully on new padded hangers, new shoes below. She went into the bathroom. Pristine and smelling of the Glade Clean Linen spray she'd bought for all the bathrooms. But, wait, beneath the air freshener there was a faint odor of charred paper. She followed it to a corner in which sat the carton Kathy had sent. Bending down, she opened the flaps. Out wafted the charred smell. She drew back, then looked closely. Books. No, a photograph album on top, and as she pried it up she saw more albums below. Photograph albums. Greg hadn't only salvaged that wedding album Kathy had brought. And Kathy must have taken possession of these too. So Kathy hadn't sent Pauline waiting-room magazines. Pauline had lied about that. And stored the carton containing a telltale odor in this air-freshened room.

Closing the flaps, Bev retreated into the bedroom and said to Dandy, "I guess Pauline is napping with photo albums. Is that a good sign?"

Dandy didn't answer. Or sing.

Then she went to fetch her shoulder bag from the kitchen and in the hallway she put on her parka and boots. Outdoors, Roger was not seen but heard; his snowblowing noise had reached the back of the house. On the cleared driveway she walked to the garage for her car.

Trapped in a nightmare.

As she drove into town, these words repeated themselves over and over in her head. Whenever she thought of the Marines trapped on Iwo Jima, the ones who hadn't been killed immediately, these were the words that came to mind. It must have been what so many of the men were thinking. But now she was applying the words to herself—and how dare she? She was safe in her peaceful hometown. The battle of Iwo Jima had lasted for five weeks of nightmare. Seven thousand Marines had died on that little island shaped like a pork chop. She was safe.

But still, the words would not go away.

On Bayview Drive the high snowbanks blanked out the view of the bay until, past the fishing-tackle store and the Twilite Motel and a closed-for-the-season gift shop, the street sloped uphill to granite gateposts that were arched over by a wrought-iron sign: Birchwood Cemetery. Now she could see the bay below, as newly white as her own East Bay, without any of the snowmobile tracks Snowy loathed. This weekend it would become looped with tracks.

The parking area had been plowed but not the wide macadam lanes on which you could cruise around the cemetery. She got out of the car and trudged past obelisks and angels and plain gravestones to the family plot. Invisible under snow were its three granite stones set flat in the ground, but of course she knew the names and dates by heart. By heart. Richard William Colby and his additional identification of U.S. Marine Corps. Julia Cushman Colby Miller. Frederick John Miller. Daddy, Mother, Fred.

She asked them aloud, "Isn't it silly of me to think I'm trapped in a nightmare?"

And then silently she asked what she always asked here. Why had her father left her and Mother and enlisted instead of waiting until older men with wives and children might be drafted? Mother had never come up with a clear answer, only saying, "It was something he felt he had to do. He was a very brave man."

Running away to war from domestic responsibilities? Choosing the Marines because they seemed to him the bravest of the brave? A more dramatic choice? Had he liked their anthem best, "From the halls of Montezuma—"?

Dramatic. *Driving Miss Daisy.* The planning meeting next week, auditions next month. The promise from Russell that she'd be Ethel in *On Golden Pond* again.

Feeling dizzy in the white light of the fresh snow, feeling weak, she turned and walked carefully back along the trail of her solidifying boot-prints.

In the car, she balked against going home and facing the rest of the day's chores. She couldn't run away to war. Visit Mimi at the Thetford store? Visit Snowy at the Woodcombe store? They were working. So should she be.

Or she could save herself some work and damn the expense. She drove to the Abnaki Mall and went in. Instead of baking the muffins and scones for the weekend, she would buy a supply.

As she stepped into Indulgences' aroma of cinnamon, pie crust, and unidentified indulgences, she saw Charl and Dudley. Delighted, she realized she hadn't seen them in ages. They were chatting with Fay, the owner, who stood behind the bountiful counter. That is, Dudley was doing the chatting, as usual. Charl's expression was oddly watchful. Fay's was patient and then relieved when she noticed Bev entering.

"Look," Fay said, interrupting Dudley, "here's Bev! It's a mini-reunion of your Gunthwaite High class!"

Dudley turned, smiling, one hand holding a small Indulgences white box by its gold cord. But there was something wrong with his eyes. Had he been drinking? He said, "Bev! My Emily! Remember when you were Emily and I was George in *Our Town*?"

She hesitated. "I certainly do."

Fay asked, "How can I help you, Bev?"

Charl said, "Come along, Dudley. Fay needs to wait on Bev."

He said to Charl, "Remember when Bev and Snowy waited on customers in Sweetland?" and explained to Fay, "Sweetland was a Main Street restaurant that isn't there anymore. I was a busboy at the Gunthwaite Inn, and it's still there."

Charl took his free hand and led him out the door.

Bev stared after them.

Fay whispered, "Alzheimer's?"

Bev could hardly comprehend the word. Then in her shoulder bag her phone began ringing. She yanked it out. Etta. She said to Fay, "I'm sorry, my daughter—could I have assorted muffins, scones, cinnamon buns, about a dozen and a half in all?" and to Etta, "Hello, darling, is everything okay? Jeremy?"

Etta exclaimed, "My agent has sold my book! I'll call you this evening with details! Bye!"

When Bev returned to her car carrying a big Indulgences box, she phoned Snowy at the Woodcombe General Store to tell her at once about Etta. Even if the Woodcombe store didn't have a lull, even if Snowy was inundated with customers, Bev wanted to make sure that she herself had been the first to learn Etta's good news, that Etta hadn't called Snowy first. But after Snowy said, "Hi, Bev," she felt speechless. Then she started to weep. She said, "I just saw Dudley and Charl at Indulgences. Snowy, you must know?"

Snowy said, "Dudley."

Bev waited. Snowy didn't continue. So Bev said, "Fay spoke the word to me. Can we say it?"

Snowy cried, "Oh, Bev, I can't bear this! *Dudley!*"

"Our Dudley. Alzheimer's."

Her voice shaky, Snowy said, "I can't even say it to Ruhamah and she hasn't to me. She's probably trying to protect me as long as possible."

"This is denial, isn't it?"

"I've been trying to preserve Dudley's dignity. Charl must be doing this too, not telling friends. She must've talked with Darl, though, mustn't she?"

"They're twins, Snowy. Maybe they don't have to talk out loud to each other."

"I haven't even spoken to Tom, to ask if he noticed, and he hasn't mentioned anything, so maybe he's trying to preserve Dudley's dignity for my sake. Bev, oh, Bev, this is terrible!"

"What do we do? How can we help? Charl and their children—D. J.—and everybody! Is Puddles well enough to be told? To see what she knows about the—the disease, about what's going to happen?"

"Dementia," Snowy said. "Things simply go downhill, don't they, despite medication?"

"What can we do?"

"Let's postpone telling Puddles." Snowy seemed to be pulling herself together. "She's just adjusting to getting back to work. But it's time for me to ask Ruhamah. It's past time. I will. Oh, excuse me, Bev." Snowy said to a customer, "Yes, February is the longest month of the year."

Bev said, "We'll talk later, bye," and as she disconnected and started searching in her shoulder bag for a Kleenex, she realized she'd forgotten to tell Snowy Etta's news. Bev would phone her tonight, after Etta called back.

Was Dudley trapped in a nightmare? Did he realize this as he tried to persevere with his usual entertaining chat?

# Chapter Seven

# 1. Snowy

Over the phone Puddles said, "The first of March and it's cold and cloudy, no snowstorm until tomorrow, so is it coming in like a lamb or a lion?" Her voice moved away from her phone but Snowy could hear her chide, "Stop singing that, Blivit, or I'll get laughing!" To Snowy she said, "He has a little ditty from his boyhood, a calypso tune about how 'man goes in like lion, comes out like lamb.'"

Snowy started laughing and leaned back in her office chair. Since she and Tom had returned home in January she had been the one to make the calls, to report any amusing happenings at the store and ask tactful questions about Puddles's recuperation. This Sunday afternoon Puddles had been the one calling, in a chatty mood. So maybe life was really returning to normal in Long Harbor. Then Snowy stopped laughing and glanced down at the March calendar and the to-do list on her desk. March 14th, the date of the store's anniversary party, had picked up speed, careening toward her.

"Men!" Puddles was saying. "Men! Did you know that nowadays guys schedule vasectomies in March so they can watch March Madness basketball games while they sit on ice packs recovering?"

"Nope, I did not know that."

"At least in March we get the official start of spring, even though that's a laugh. But would you believe I'm thinking ahead to next winter? I'm going to see if I can make our geraniums live on through the winter. The way my mother did in Maine and New Hampshire."

"What a fun challenge, Puddles." Winter's challenges. The canceled reading at the Midhurst library had been rescheduled for April when everyone hoped there wouldn't be another snowstorm. Geraniums; plants; gardening. Snowy glanced out the window at the garden under snow. She thought of those farmers and farmwives who'd come to the opening of the first Woodcombe General Store worrying about the work of the spring planting. It dawned on her that she herself had a choice; her gardening wasn't a necessity. She could reduce its size this year. Hell, if she wanted to, she could just have a tomato plant and herbs in pots on the picnic table. Talk about lazy beds! Startled, she realized that the idea of retiring from gardening seemed to be causing more relief than regret. And then she thought of the love-seat-style settee Tom had built last year for a Valentine present, on which she had sat last summer to rest her back during work in the garden. Hell, again! She could still sit there to rest in general, couldn't she?

Puddles was saying something that ended with "—and March means you'll turn seventy."

"Remember," she replied, "the store is even older, it's turning a hundred and fifty, so I'm eclipsed, a youngster."

Puddles said, as she'd said before, "Wish I could be at the anniversary party, but we've got a game that Saturday."

"I wish you could too. But right this very minute I'll let you in on Ruhamah's plans for a surprise announcement at the cake-cutting ceremony the afternoon of the party. The town selectmen—well, two are women—are presenting an anniversary plaque to us and then Ruhamah will announce our—her—big decision: putting wood-fired pizza ovens in all three stores."

"Holy shit. But aren't pizzas a hassle?"

"That's why we've avoided them."

"Needs must," said Puddles.

"Well, anyway, Bev can't come either. The Inn at East Bay is definitely going to be full and she'll be too busy. But she's represented by her meat-loaf recipe in the cookbook."

"Have you got the cookbook finished?"

"It's at the printer's in Vermont now and supposedly they're shipping it to us tomorrow, so it'll get here in plenty of time for the party. I don't know what we'll do if it doesn't. The cookbook is the highlight of the party; we're serving samples from it." Her editing work might be finished but worries remained. Oh, the stress after the point-of-no-return with a book, be it a collection of poems or recipes! What if she'd missed even one teeny-tiny typo in the galleys or one wrong measurement number, ten teaspoons of salt instead of one?

"Speaking of books," Puddles said, "any more news about when the publisher will have Etta's book out?"

It was such a relief that *Boot, Saddle, to Horse, and Away* would be published. After telling Snowy last month, Bev (via Etta) had given Snowy permission to tell Puddles about Etta's murder mystery. And Etta had e-mailed Snowy permission to pass along the printout to Bev (in which Bev had learned that the heroine's mother was never mentioned, and Bev hadn't seemed insulted by the maternal omission, whew!). "No more details yet," Snowy said. "These things always take longer than you think they will, even in the computer age." She paused. If life was really settling down for Puddles, was this the right moment to speak about Dudley? Could she, without crying? She drew a deep breath. "But Puddles, there *is* some other news. Sad news. About Dudley. He's not—himself. Ruhamah and D. J. have been keeping tabs for some time. Charl finally got Dudley to the doctor, and they went too, along with Darl. They all went to Dudley and Charl's primary-care doctor." She paused again.

Puddles said, "Snowy, spit it out."

"Dudley took a memory test in the doctor's office, and then the doctor had an appointment made for him with a mental-health counselor. They went and she—the counselor—tentatively diagnosed dementia. Alzheimer's. So now they're waiting to get an appointment with a neurologist."

"Which," said Puddles in her professional voice, "will probably take a while." Then she wailed, "Oh, goddamnit all to fucking hell! Dudley, not Dudley!" A phone rang in the background. Puddles yelled, "Blivit, don't answer your cell, Snowy just told me—I want to tell you—!" She stopped. "Shit, too late, he's answered it. Snowy, Alzheimer's can hit anybody. But—*Dudley*?"

"What happens?" Snowy asked. "I've made myself Google at last, but have you known anybody, have any of the patients at your clinic had it?"

"Early, before they go on to doctors in Fort George. Wait, Blivit is saying something—huh? The call is from Aunt Izzy?" Murmur from Blivit. Puddles said, "Oh, my God. Mildred Cotter has died. At the rehab place."

Snowy froze. "Mildred?"

"I'll call you back later." Puddles disconnected.

Mildred Cotter, Snowy thought. She should go tell Tom. But she sat there. A strange sort of shock and grief. They'd only met Mildred twice, for brief conversations; no, those could hardly be called conversations. But during the two weeks in her cottage they'd been completely in her presence, amid her belongings, the stuff of her island days: the Blue Willow dishes and the glass dishes shaped like fish in the kitchen cupboards, the 1950s pink tub and basin and toilet in the bathroom, the Gauguin and Seurat prints on a living-room wall showing, respectively, Tahiti and an island in the Seine. The bedroom bookcase's collection of Mary Stewart novels. And Snowy had found in the bottom drawer of the bureau a map of Indonesia. Also a Virgin Islands map of St. Thomas circled by a green vine with white flowers, pretty calligraphy explaining, "The Love Vine. Considered an aphrodisiac, it is a parasite that kills the host plant. The love vine kills what it embraces." When Snowy had asked Aunt Izzy and Florence, her granddaughter, about the maps, she'd learned that Mildred had wanted to leave Quarry Island and see far-flung islands but had only got as far away as Maine's mainland. Florence had said, "The failure soured her." Snowy hadn't told them about the love vine, but when she and Tom had visited Mildred that first time at the rehab place Snowy had mentioned seeing the St. Thomas map with the vine decoration. Mildred had said, "It kills what it embraces. You don't have to go to St. Thomas to encounter the love vine. You can have your heart broken anywhere. Your spirit broken. Killed. Even in Portland, Maine." And Snowy had said, knowing the words inadequate, "I'm so sorry. So sorry."

She went into the kitchen, where Tom, in his parka, was lining the two tall wastebaskets with new empty trash bags. The full bags leaned against the door.

He said, "I guess I'm all set. Want to come along?"

His weekly trip to the dump. She should stay and concentrate on her to-do list. The party preparations. But she said, "Yes," sat down in a kitchen chair, took off her shoes, donned her boots. He brought her parka. As he helped her on with it, she touched his hands and held them against her shoulders. "Tom, you heard the phone? That was Puddles, and in the midst of the call Blivit had a call from Aunt Izzy. Mildred, Tom. Mildred has died."

He gathered her into his arms. "Damn."

"I don't know why it's such a shock."

"Because she was feisty?" He hugged her.

Then he picked up the full bags, and Snowy followed him down the stairs, outdoors to his black Ford Ranger. Main

Street dozed in this dull afternoon. He hoisted the bags into the pickup's bed, which already held bags of the workshop's weekly accumulation.

As they drove out of the village, she said, "I should write a sympathy letter, but to whom? Aunt Izzy, yes, but also to somebody in Mildred's family? Her nieces and nephews—we've never met them. Roddy, though, is Mildred's grandnephew."

"Writing Aunt Izzy should be sufficient."

But Snowy resolved to write Florence and Roddy.

He turned onto Phinney Road and drove past the converted barn in which Fay and her husband lived. Snowy remembered how Ruhamah had taken refuge there with Fay's family after Alan's death, for which Ruhamah blamed Snowy. History everywhere. She thought of Cotter Cottage and Mildred's history. Aunt Izzy had arranged the renting of two weeks in their new cottage, Sea-Fever, and Snowy had sent a check to the owner, Jerome Morris, feeling somehow unfaithful. When she and Tom were staying there in May, would they go have a look at Cotter Cottage, the cottage to which Mildred hadn't returned after all?

On the left a road sign appeared: Woodcombe Transfer Station. The modern name for a dump. The dump road through woods was paved but narrow, and in winter, with snowbanks, you slowed down and squeezed carefully past any oncoming vehicles, or at least prudent people did. Tom did. Sundays were apt to be busy, though not so busy now as in summer. Tom's pickup joined the little line parked near the shed containing the bins with signs stating their purposes: Household Trash. Recyclables. Cardboard.

She remembered Bev's telling her about Lloyd's discovery of Mrs. Pollifax at the Leicester dump and his subsequent romance with her. Woodcombe's dump also had a Swap Shop, in which Snowy and Tom had browsed and to which they'd occasionally contributed, but she'd avoided the books section for fear of finding one or more of her own books discarded there. Today, however, as Tom began unloading the pickup she strolled toward the Swap Shop shed, away from the ripe smell of Household Trash. Maybe she'd find a Mary Stewart.

Ryan Hopkins's heavy-duty truck approached, its bed crowded with garbage cans topped by bulging trash bags lolling precariously. He was known for not bothering to go to the dump often enough. He lowered his window. "Is the cookbook back from the printer?"

"They're shipping tomorrow."

He beamed, gave her a thumbs-up, and drove on to join the line. He'd been dumbstruck when she'd suggested he contribute his Welsh Rabbit recipe. Years earlier, while he was buying a pound of cheese he had mentioned that his method of making Welsh Rabbit (no "Rarebit" nonsense from Ryan) consisted of just loosening the cheese with beer, and she said that she made it the same way. At her cookbook suggestion, he protested that she should write up the recipe—or wasn't it too simple to be a recipe? She'd replied that recipes could be simple and anyway, she was already contributing the Woodcombe General Store's corn chowder recipe. So he'd agreed, flattered.

Were townsfolk getting in a party mood?

Inside the Swap Shop, items that belonged in homes looked cold and abandoned, amongst them a rocking horse and an ironing board and, on the rudimentary shelves, a painted vase, five matching highball glasses, pots and pans, canning jars, and books, mostly paperbacks. She scanned bindings. None of her books. But—an Agatha Christie! And it was *The Mysterious Affair at Styles*, Agatha's first! She grabbed it. She already had a copy, of course, but she would someday give it to Al and keep this copy. She didn't have anything to swap today; she would bring some book next time. Perhaps a collection by Henrietta Snow.

Would she be able get through the party without crying? Twenty-four years ago she and Alan had bought the old rundown store. How hard he had worked to revive it! While she, hamstrung by agoraphobia, had been hardly of any help at all.

Finished unloading the pickup, Tom waved to her.

She waved Agatha and hurried back. Home to her to-do list.

## 2. Snowy

Saturday, March 14th at last, and the store was in a tizzy as the morning began, customers arriving early. Today Snowy had jazzed up one of her usual blue Woodcombe General

Store sweatshirts with a present Harriet had brought her from a trip to Israel, a silk scarf hand-painted with splashes of pink, gold, blue, purple, green, and turquoise. She fussed again over the stacks of cookbooks arranged on a table carried up from the storeroom, feeling almost as if she were at one of her book signings, though all the contributors would be signing if asked to. When she glanced out the store's windows at the dawning sun that was making the 10° weather appear warmer, she could see the back of the banner strung across the porch and knew that the other side said 150TH ANNIVERSARY CELEBRATION, MARCH 14! She remembered walking to the store with Tom last June on their wedding day and seeing the banner that David and Lavender had strung there; it said FINALLY!

She laughed and tried to relax. The cookbooks were here and, knock on wood, she hadn't found any errors when she pored over the first copy of the first carton in fear and trembling. But relax? At the lunch counter, Ruhamah and Rita were busy serving the samples made by some of the people who'd contributed breakfast recipes to the cookbook, Rita extolling the scrumptiousness of her banana bread. D. J., home from Washington for the occasion, was partly helping and partly tending to Al, who watched raptly from his baby carrier set in a counter corner.

Then she saw Patsy Fletcher cross the porch carrying a plastic-wrapped plate and pause to hold the door open for Woodcombe's centenarian, Gladys Stanton. Eagerly they both approached the book table, Patsy exclaiming, "The cookbook!"

Snowy held up two copies, cover outward to show them its historical society photo of this store in its earlier days. Contributors got free copies. "The finished product, and here are yours. Thank you again, Gladys, Patsy."

Gladys's recipe was for dandelion wine. Snowy watched her set down her purse and open her copy slowly—reverently?—and then skim down the Table of Contents to "Beverages" and quickly turn pages. Lloyd had designed an array of beverage glasses for the section-divider page. Gladys stopped and studied it. Then she turned to the next page, on which hers was the first recipe. She read aloud, "'Two quarts of dandelion blossoms picked when the sun is on them. Plunge into boiling water before they are wilted.'" She looked up. "I used to send the children out on a May morning to pick them. Two quarts of blossoms are a *lot* to pick on your own."

Patsy remarked, "I'd've had to pay my kids to do that."

"Well," Gladys said, "I must admit that in later years when the children were grown and gone, I paid the neighborhood children."

Patsy waved to Ruhamah and said to Snowy, "I'll drop off my macaroons with Ruhamah for the lunch crowd, say hello to Al and D. J., and be on my way. Nelson has an appointment in Gunthwaite this morning with our eye doctor, who thinks he'll need cataract surgery in the near future. Aging sure is fun, isn't it, Gladys?"

"Consider the alternative," Gladys said, stroking the book.

They laughed. Patsy said, "The book is beautiful, Snowy," and hurried over to the counter.

Gladys mused, "The one-hundred-and-fiftieth anniversary. I remember when Joshua Bickford's son had the first gas pump put in. Thank you for keeping the store going this long."

Oh, no, Snowy thought, Gladys is going to start me crying.

"And now," Gladys said, "I'll partake of some coffee and one of those interesting-looking lavender muffins on the counter. From our Lavender Forbes, I assume?"

"Her lemon-lavender muffins." David's wife enjoyed all the possibilities of her name. "In her recipe she explains fine-tuning the food coloring."

"More blue than red, no doubt. Let's hope so in politics too." Gladys picked up her purse and, holding the cookbook to her bosom, went to the counter.

Maybe, Snowy thought, searching the pockets of her jeans for a Kleenex, maybe Joshua Bickford had been afraid of failure when he started the store, but he had succeeded. Alan had nearly failed. She and Ruhamah had been trying their best, and Gladys had thanked her for keeping the heart of the village beating. They'd done so here and in Thetford and Oakhill. But for how long could they? Could they be saved by pizza? She saw Kyle, the police chief, waiting at the checkout counter with his coffee and what was left of a slice of banana bread, and went across to the cash register.

And as the morning progressed, while she moved back and forth between the cash register and the book table, making change, making conversation, occasionally signing a book, she sensed a special hum in the store that felt different from the Saturday weekend-relaxation of the customers. It was a celebration.

Midmorning, D. J. took Al home. A lull. Ruhamah got the corn chowder going. Rita tidied up.

Then in strode Ryan Hopkins. "Where are the cookbooks—there they are! Well, by God, they *are* a book, a real book!"

"It's always a miracle." Snowy handed him a copy. "Here is yours, with our thanks."

He opened it. "My recipe is really in here?"

"In the Eggs and Cheese section."

He flipped pages, stopped, stared. "I'll be damned." He laughed. "I'll be damned!"

The door opened. Harriet and Jared! As Harriet had promised, she had come up from New York for this. Snowy left Ryan and ran to hug them. Harriet said, "Happy hundred-fiftieth anniversary!" She was sporting her New Hampshire attire, parka and flannel shirt and jeans; so was Woodcombe-native Jared but he did not look chic. Then Harriet said, "The cookbook!" and made a beeline to the table, where Ryan was still gazing in wonder at his recipe. Over the years Harriet had become acquainted with some of the Woodcombe folks, and she said, "Hi there, Ryan," before she picked up a copy and called to Jared, "Come see your recipe, Jared!"

Ryan glanced up. He and Jared exchanged a silent male message. Embarrassed? Ironic? Master-chef-like?

Jared said to him, "Mine's trout."

At Harriet's house Snowy and Tom had dined on Jared's fresh-caught trout several times, so Snowy had suggested and Harriet had insisted he contribute his recipe.

"Mine's Welsh Rabbit," Ryan said. "Made with beer."

Harriet had opened the copy and was paging through. "There's a fish section. Here it is."

Snowy had been glad that Lloyd had illustrated the divider page with a trout, even though most of the recipes were for tuna and salmon.

Harriet said, "Doesn't this trout look tempting," and gave Snowy a female glance that meant Jared had also looked tempting when Harriet had first set eyes on the young carpenter with his big—ahem!—tape measure on his belt, right here in this store nineteen years ago.

Snowy couldn't help giggling. "And fishing season starts next month."

"Coffee," Jared said, starting for the counter.

Ryan asked Snowy, "Did you say there'd be cake? One of Fay's cakes?"

"I'm sorry, you're too early. We'll be cutting the cake at two o'clock this afternoon. But now there might be some coffee cake left."

"Gotcha," Ryan said and joined Jared.

Harriet said reminiscently, "Coffee Cake Therapy."

Snowy too recalled their favorite Bennington breakfast, a treat that put scholarly endeavor in perspective. She said, "Those were the days."

"I like your scarf."

"So do I. An old school chum gave it to me."

They smiled at each other, and Harriet resumed turning pages. "Mimi's husband has done a great job. Maybe freelancing might be his full-time answer."

"It may have to be." Then Snowy realized that Harriet dealt with printed matter, her gallery's various brochures and publications. Maybe Harriet was thinking Lloyd could handle the designing of something of hers?

Harriet closed the book. "So, have you decided how to celebrate your seventieth?"

Like Bev and Puddles, Harriet was a youngster. Harriet wouldn't turn seventy until August. Snowy said, "Thursday is a workday and there'll probably be a snowstorm so I'm thinking of postponing my birthday until May and celebrating it on Tom's birthday. I'll be like Queen Elizabeth with two birthdays—"

All of a sudden, Tom was in the store in a gust of cold air, his parka unzipped, his face flushed, and he was grabbing her hand. "Come out on the porch!"

"Tom," she said, "what's the matter? Al?"

"No, no." He tugged her out the door.

The porch was empty and the sun had not warmed it. She said, "My parka—"

He put his arms around her, tucking her into his parka. "Aunt Izzy just phoned with a piece of information. How she found out she wouldn't say, but Aunt Izzy knows everything that goes on, doesn't she."

Her voice muffled, Snowy said, "Yes, but what—?"

"Aunt Izzy thought we should be forewarned so the shock wouldn't kill us. Remember, she or Blivit told us last year how Mildred worked for ages at that law firm in Portland?"

"Yes."

"So of course she has a will. She must've changed it sometime in the past year. Maybe in the past couple of months. She left the cottage to us."

"*Tom.*"

He laughed. "I was so dumbstruck I didn't even think to ask Aunt Izzy what the hell the property taxes are like on Quarry Island."

"What about Roddy? Shouldn't he inherit?"

"I didn't think to ask that either, but Aunt Izzy said right away we shouldn't worry about Roddy, the last thing he wants is another house on the island."

And, nearly pole-axed, Snowy thought: It's Tom. Mildred must have left the cottage to Tom, not to Tom and me; if I'm named, I'm incidental. Old ladies, as he himself had said, liked Tom.

## 3. Bev

OPENING THE DOOR OF WOOD DUCK, BEV CHECKED HER WATCH. Yes, at Snowy's store the cake-cutting ceremony was going on now, with an Indulgences creation that Snowy had described to her over the phone yesterday, a big sheet cake, the store's sign piped in white and black onto the background of optimistically springtime-green frosting. Bev wanted to be there, not standing in this doorway looking at the guest room that had been her home office.

But here she was, snooping. On Thursday Pauline had announced that her daughter had phoned and would be coming to Gunthwaite on Saturday—and, since Wood Duck was the one room that hadn't been reserved for this weekend, Pauline had decided Kathy would stay in Wood Duck, where she'd stayed at Christmas. Had Pauline consulted Roger? Oh, who cared! But Bev was curious to see if, while helping to ready the guest rooms, Pauline had added special touches for Kathy.

No, Pauline hadn't put any charred family photos on the bureau. The bedside table held only the lamp with ducks flying around its lampshade. Bev crossed to the bathroom. The usual duck towels. The rubber ducky on the vanity wasn't a new whimsical touch from Pauline; she herself had bought it to show Roger that if he wanted to name her office Wood Duck, she would take his bright idea to the extreme. Actually, the rubber ducky had been a fun purchase, full of memories of her children in the bathtub. It hadn't been the scary purchase that the expensive bed linens and towels had been.

Why was Kathy coming? Pauline had just said that Kathy wanted to show her something. Another photo album?

Bev moved to where her desk had stood and looked out the window at the backyard still deep in snow. Each spring after she had put the loon whirligig on the lawn, from this window she would watch the loon flapping and it would aid her thinking, her work. All the work she had done in this room over the years!

She spun around and left, then slowly went downstairs. This weekend's six guests, including Lydia and Trent—and Walter and the Grace who'd admired Harriet's painting in the dining room—were at the ski area. Pauline was in her room. Roger was in the cellar, something about "bait stations" for mice. Could she briefly pretend that Waterlight was hers again?

Hearing a car door slam, she went into the hallway. Out the window she saw Kathy standing next to a car. But Kathy was on the passenger side. Then a man got out of the driver's side. The car, she realized, had New York license plates. They hadn't flown; they'd driven.

Greg. The man was Kathy's father, looming broad and bulky in his parka.

Bev ran to Pauline's room and banged on the door. "Pauline! Kathy's here!"

Pauline seemed to take forever to open the door. "She's early. She must've made good time from the airport."

"She didn't fly." Bev paused. "She brought someone with her and he drove."

"Who?"

"Greg."

Pauline stared at her. "Oh, shit." She slammed the door.

Bev stood there.

Kathy called, "Mom? Uncle Roger? Aunt Bev?"

What to do? Bev called back, "We're here! Pauline's room!"

She heard muttering and sounds that could be the coat closet's door opening and closing. Then down the corridor came Kathy and Greg, Kathy disconcerting her again by looking a little like Roger and Leon. Kathy wasn't wearing a dress this time; instead, jeans and a nice black sweater. In addition to her pocketbook she was carrying a small manila envelope. Behind her, his expression wary, Greg was wearing clothes that appeared to be newish: a quilted blue vest, blue sweatshirt, and jeans. His remaining hair had gone grayer since she'd last seen him.

Bev automatically smiled and greeted them with, "Hello, welcome!" Where the hell would they put Greg? Pauline wouldn't allow him to stay in her room, that was certain. Gesturing at the barrier of the door, Bev made a helpless face and told Kathy, "I mentioned your father was with you."

Kathy called, "Mom, open up! I've got something to show you!"

Pauline yelled, "I know what you brought! Him!"

"Mom, it's something we both want to show you. To *give* you."

Behind the door, Dandy made conversational noises.

Pauline opened the door, ignored Greg, and looked only at Kathy, who took out of the envelope—what? Photographs rescued from the fire? But they didn't seem charred.

"What's that?" Pauline asked.

Kathy replied, "The ultrasound prints, Mom. Tanya and Shane are having a baby."

Tanya. Bev remembered this was Kathy's daughter's name.

Greg finally spoke. "A boy. Our first great-grandchild, Pauline."

Kathy said, "I've got images on my phone, too."

Time to leave them alone. Bev hurried away down the corridor, marveling over the power of grandchildren and great-grandchildren. She herself had bought Bide-a-Wee with its small engine repairs shop because of a grandson. As she reached the hallway she heard another car door slam shut. Prospective customers? No rooms available!

Looking outdoorsy, Lydia and Trent came in, unzipping their ski jackets.

Lydia said, "Hi, Bev, we were hoping to catch you when you had a spare moment. Is this a good time?"

Eek, did they have a complaint? She'd always remembered lactose-free offerings. Or—oh, God, did they want to talk to her about Lydia's grandfather? Dudley, dearest Dudley. "Yes," she said, "it's fine."

Trent said, "We'd planned to wait and see about buying a second home until after we'd started a family, but we've changed our minds. Life is short."

Lydia said, "We decided not to waste any more time."

Stunned, Bev thought: Maybe we *are* talking about Dudley. Then she thought: There must be more money on Trent's side than a professor's salary! Even in this recession.

Lydia added, "And everyone says you're the best realtor around."

Bev gasped, "I—I'd be delighted to help, what do you have in mind, would you like to come to my office this afternoon and discuss things, start looking at listings, or do it tomorrow?" Calm down, she admonished herself. Keep calm and carry on.

Trent repeated, "Life is short," and re-zipped his jacket. "Let's go to your office."

Bev said, "I'll just tell Roger I'm leaving," and made herself walk, not run, to the kitchen. She opened the cellar door. "Roger?"

No answer.

She went down the stairs and peered into the granite cellar's depths, past the freezer and the shelves of canned goods and the soapstone sink. The cellar was so big that it had easily accommodated the accumulated junk of previous generations when she bought the place, and she hadn't added much. But with Roger's arrival it began to get cramped; now, in its B-and-B era, it was crammed, especially with the leftovers from renovations that Roger had saved, from cans containing a dab of paint to seemingly useless slabs of wallboard. She saw him near the furnace and oil tank, sitting in the old armchair left by somebody. He was—simply asleep, wasn't he? She tiptoed forward. He was breathing.

He looked worn out. He looked seventy-two years old.

Why in the world was she suddenly thinking of F. Scott Fitzgerald right now? A note from Fitzgerald's notebooks—yes, Snowy had quoted it at the start of a poem in one of her collections. Snowy had been writing about the vulnerability of sleep. And, unlike the poem itself, this quotation had stuck in Bev's memory as if it were a line in a script: *She was asleep—he stood for a moment beside the bed, sorry for her, because she was asleep, and because she had set her slippers beside her bed.*

She bent and lightly kissed the top of his head. He grunted but didn't wake up. She tiptoed back to the stairs. She too would write a note, and she would leave it on Roger's desk, a note saying she'd gone to her office.

Scripts. Friday evening she would go to the summer theater's planning meeting.

## 4. Bev

THURSDAY WAS SNOWY'S BIRTHDAY, AND AS BEV PULLED INTO the parking lot of her grandson's elementary school in the north end of town at 10:15 that morning she saw Snowy's car already here. Of course Snowy would be on time. Bev was a little late, having detoured to her office with her laptop, to check her e-mail in private. She parked beside Snowy, who was gazing straight ahead out the windshield. Was Snowy actually taking in the scene on this cloudy day, the one-story brick building and the playground amid snowbanks tired out from too much winter, neighborhood houses on either side and woods behind, or was she daydreaming about the Maine cottage that, as she'd told Bev when Bev phoned Saturday night to ask about the store's party, she and Tom had apparently inherited?

Snowy turned, waved, and began getting out of her car.

Bev was faster and hugged her. "Happy birthday, septuagenarian!"

"Good morning, you young whippersnapper."

They laughed. Then they both looked at the school. Nowadays, Bev thought, all the town's elementary schools were like this, the old big brick ones having been renovated into office buildings, including the school across town in which they'd met at age seven. From seven to seventy, how utterly incomprehensible!

Snowy asked, "Where is Clem's sap house?"

"Out back." Bev led the way across the parking lot toward the cleared path around the playground. During that Saturday phone call she had learned that Snowy still was planning to do nothing special on her birthday, so Bev had reminded her that it was sap season and insisted she at least take the morning off and they would meet here to visit the new sap house in action and buy some maple syrup from the kids. Who could resist fresh maple syrup? Not Snowy. Bev asked, "Is there any update about the cottage?"

Snowy stopped.

When she'd told Bev the news she had sounded as dazed as somebody who'd won the lottery. Bev realized she looked rather shell-shocked.

"It's official," Snowy said. "Yesterday the letter from the lawyer arrived. Aunt Izzy's information was accurate. But even with the letter, we can't quite believe it."

"What are you going to do?"

"We're still trying to figure out if we can afford to keep it. Us, with a cottage, a 'second home'? Doesn't seem possible."

On Saturday Bev hadn't told Snowy (or Roger) about Lydia and Trent, fearing it would jinx the possibilities. Could she today, after Lydia's e-mail this morning confirming their decision to buy the winterized cottage on Hidden Harbor? No, not until it was really and truly final. But she had told Snowy about Greg and Kathy's visit, with Greg taking Pauline out for a drive and dinner. And Sunday evening Bev had phoned Snowy again, to report that Greg had spent last night in Pauline's room and Pauline had announced this morning that she was going to pack her basics and leave today with Greg and Kathy; the rest should be sent. Pauline and Dandy would be going back home, to Greg's condo.

Bev said, "A 'second home.' I can't handle our *only* home. Roger has had another of his brainstorms: come spring, he wants to put in one of those fire-pit rings."

"A fire pit on your lawn?"

"So the guests can sit around it in the evenings with their drinks, talking and toasting marshmallows. He says we should think of our guests as our extended family. I suppose the smoke will discourage the blackflies and mosquitoes."

Snowy giggled.

Bev resumed walking, Snowy following, alongside empty swing sets and a jungle gym. Then children's voices could be heard ahead where against the woods stood the sap house that Leon had built. Steam flowed up from its metal chimney. Throughout her life Bev had gone to Gunthwaite sap houses, with Mother, with Leon and Etta after moving back here from Connecticut, and later on her own, most recently with

Clem. Those sap houses were aged, their rough-board exteriors weathered gray. This one's exterior was new and blond, and sap houses were called sugarhouses or sugar shacks nowadays.

Snowy said, "Look at the kids!"

Three bundled-up kids trudged out of the woods along a tramped-down path through the snow, talking excitedly, each lugging a metal pail. Bev and Snowy halted and watched.

Bev said, "I've forgotten how many maples Clem told me they've tapped this first year—oh, there's the last on this trip."

The kids had stopped at a maple tree at the edge of the woods. One of them lifted down the smaller pail hanging beneath the metal tap and poured sap into his pail. Then they continued onward to the sap house.

Snowy said, "In the historical society's booklets, I've read that a gallon of syrup was worth a man's daily pay. Farmers traded syrup at the store. Will the kids have doughnuts on hand, the way some regular sap houses do?"

"Oh, yes." Bev took the path across the snow-mounded playing field. As they neared the sap house she saw a hand-lettered sign on the door that said: We're Boiling!

"Two beautiful words," Snowy said.

When they entered, the place suddenly didn't seem new to Bev. It seemed familiar and snug with its steamy warmth and the sweet-*sweet*-SWEET smell of boiling sap. Kids were clustered around the huge flat evaporating pan presided over by Clem and also by a teacher, Peter Harrison, who had grown up on a farm tapping trees and thus had volunteered to oversee this project; he was explaining the syrup-making process to his young audience. Bev smiled at Clem, and Clem nodded. Then, so as not to embarrass him by hovering, she moved past the group to the back wall where on a shelf several plastic jugs of maple syrup were displayed, half-pints, pints, and quarts. On a table, little paper cups held samples and there was a large box of Dunkin' Donuts Munchkins beside them; Snowy zeroed in.

Lowering her voice, Bev said, "I asked Clem if they'd be making maple-sugar candies and he said no, that's too much, so I'll go to my usual sap house for those as well as some more syrup. Maple candies will be a nice touch for the guests, and God knows the guests partake of plenty of syrup."

Dunking a Munchkin, Snowy said, "Last Sunday I went with Tom again on his dump run and as we went past the Rollinses' house I remembered the time Fay threw a pajama party for mothers there, remember?"

"Years and years ago."

"It occurred to me that you have the perfect place for a grandmothers' pajama party for you and me and Puddles and Charl and Darl and who else?"

Astounded, Bev said, "A pajama party for grandmothers?"

"For the Gang. In the off-season, if there aren't any guests. Except that it would be like a busman's holiday for you. Without Pauline to help you and Miranda, you're going to be out straight, aren't you, even in the off-season."

"Snowy, I do not know how I'm going to manage."

"It was just a silly thought." Snowy popped the Munchkin in her mouth.

Peter Harrison said, "Okay, time for sampling," and, herded by him, the kids headed for the table. Bev waved to Peter, grabbed a quart of syrup, still warm in its jug, Snowy grabbed another one, and they squeezed past the kids, back to Clem at the cash box. Bev refrained from hugging him. A small hand-lettered sign listed prices: quarts cost $15.

Snowy took her wallet out of her shoulder bag. "Clem, this sap house is great. Maple syrup is so full of history, it's educational."

"And it's environmental," Clem said, "and ecological." He grinned. "And I get to stay outdoors a lot."

As they paid, Bev told him, "I'll be spending the rest of the day at my office, so I'll see you after school."

"Sure," he said.

They walked to the parking lot, cradling the warm syrup jugs like babies. Bev remembered last October when she'd phoned Snowy in tears about frogs and other creatures drowning in the septic-system hole and Snowy had immediately come to Waterlight—the Inn at East Bay—to see the renovations. Bev had feared not surviving the winter. But Roger's harebrained scheme had kept the bills paid. For how long? Well, the sap was now running in the maples and tomorrow would be the first day of spring.

When they reached their cars she said, "Even if Roger says we can't afford it, I'll insist we hire somebody to help out, sort of replace Pauline. So let's think about a grandmothers' pajama party."

"Really?"

"Wait'll we tell Puddles!"

They laughed, hugged, got into their cars, and drove back to work.